girlsgoneastray

girlsgoneastray

short & shorter stories

susan isa efros

To Maria,
instant love connection
♡ !
Enjoy !
Susan
7/2.1

Polished Stone Publishing
P.O. Box 2202
Sebastopol, CA 95473

Cover design and interior layout by Lesley Thornton-Raymond
Cover art by Jerilyn Gilbert
Art direction by Katherine Dieter

"The Hoarder" was originally published in *Narrative Magazine*.
"On the Bench" was originally published in *Ascent*.
"Vegetables" first appeared under the title "Welcome to America" in *Footwork: The Paterson Literary Review*.
"Amends" first appeared under the title "Shame" in *Amelia*.
"Visiting Bobby" and "Saying Goodbye" were originally published in *Christopher Street*.
"Uncle Sammy" was originally published in *Paris Transcontinental*.
"Footface" was originally published in *Juked*.

ISBN: 978-0-9980976-0-2

First Printing
Printed in the USA on acid free paper
10 9 8 7 6 5 4 3 2 1

Dedicated to Reid and Lane

Contents

Acknowledgments

My thanks to my mentors, Carol, Tom and Jane at *Narrative*. Also to my early readers and dearest friends, Sandy, Fritzi, Cynthia, Margy, Deb, Susan, Margie, Clare and Michael P. To the brilliant women in my writers' group: Sam, Jenny and KD. To Leslie Keenan for her early encouragement. And to David Haydon for his mega-generosity.

To Leah for all her computer wizardry, for building my website and for spreading the word; to Marleen for sending out my stories, and to Katherine, my amazing editor and publisher; to my loving sister, Lynda, and my remarkable niece, Marlee; to Michelle, Manuela, Arina, Carolyn, Debra, Mary, Christine, Gretchen, Tim and especially Caroline, who have helped keep me in sound mind and body throughout the process of writing this book.

And finally, to my beloved partner of thirty years, Jerie Gilbert, who is also my best friend, my editor, my illustrator, my cook, and my greatest fan.

Sea Lion

On the Saturday my father got robbed, he called my mother from his shop to tell her the sons of bitches had clipped him for twelve Hoover uprights while he was in the toilet. Then he told her he was on his way home and didn't want any extra commotion when he got there. By five o'clock my mother had lined up the pickled herring jar, toothpicks, Planter's Deluxe Mixed Nuts, and a shot of bourbon on a TV tray in the den where he watched the news before dinner. She took her Valium, and reminded my eleven-year-old wimpy brother Marky and me, just turned fifteen, not to be rambunctious. Then she began to hum.

My mother focused on problems as little as possible, believing that eventually everything would get better on its own. My father, however, took trouble as a personal affront, and believed it was up to him to fix whatever went wrong. He could go from euphoric over a Dodger victory to enraged over something as stupid as a broken radio.

You could sense what kind of mood he was in even before you saw him. If he was whistling, we were in luck, but the screeching of the Oldsmobile's wheels in the driveway and the violent stabbing of his keys in the front door lock indicated that some rotten customer had given him a hard time, or decided to take his goddamned business to Sears. This lousy situation, my father informed us, was what the owner of a small appliance shop in West Los Angeles constantly had to contend with to make a living. This time, however, criminals were involved.

"If I'd come out front one minute earlier, I could have been killed," my father barked when he came into the kitchen. I was setting the table and knew better than to look up.

"But you didn't and you weren't, so calm yourself, Irving. You'll have a heart attack," my mother said through her afternoon haze of Valium.

"Calm myself? Are you out of your mind Rachel? Did you hear what I just said? I was almost murdered!" Swinging his arm in the air, he bumped the toaster and it crashed to the floor. "Who in the hell put the toaster so close to the edge?" he yelled, and kicked it across the room. It made an impressive dent in the wall. Then he slammed the kitchen door so hard the Fiesta plates on the Formica table rattled for several seconds before they came to a rest.

Instead of retreating to the den as usual, my father headed for the garage to ride his stationary bike. My mother sat at the kitchen table, and washed down a second pill with her leftover cup of cold coffee. Then she turned to me. "Tell your brother that dinner is in fifteen minutes. Go wash up. And Shelley, don't do anything to aggravate him tonight."

I thought everyone in my family was nuts. My father was the ape in charge of the money. My mother was the nervous bird flying around the house pecking at dirt and dust, making everything neat and clean and polished so she didn't have to think about what a lunatic my father was and how chaotic our lives were. My brother was the frightened mouse, always nibbling at his fingers like they were made out of cheese. And he had the worst overbite, until he got his braces. Bullies at school called him a fag, which made Marky throw up a lot. No way I wanted to be associated with him. I was the octopus with eight fists tightly clenched, ready to punch anyone who messed with me or tried to stop me from escaping the family nuthouse when I graduated from high school in two years.

At dinner my father stabbed at his pot roast, gulped his root beer and stared intensely at the ketchup bottle. Maybe he was imagining being shot, lying on the floor of his appliance shop with blood pouring out of his guts.

"You'll feel better tomorrow, Irv," my mother tried to hypnotize him. "Once we get on the road, you'll relax and forget about everything that happened today. Thank god you weren't hurt."

"Whatever," my father said, hunched over his plate like a baboon.

Every Sunday, no matter what, our family drove along the Pacific Coast Highway to Malibu to the Sea Lion Restaurant for a family dinner. My mother equated family togetherness, even happiness, with this particular restaurant.

"As you know, kids, your father got robbed today which was very traumatic," she said. "He deserves a peaceful weekend after such a miserable week. Tomorrow is his day!"

"Okay, Mommy!" Marky piped up, exposing his rabbit teeth.

"That's my guy," my mother said, tousling his curly hair.

"Can I be excused?" I asked. "I have a ton of homework." I'd heard enough crap for one night.

The next morning I snuck into Marky's room while he was in the shower and snatched "Jailhouse Rock" from his Elvis collection of 45s. He never lent me anything, so I thought it was my responsibility to teach him the virtue of sharing. I took his records to avenge his stinginess. This time he walked in on me.

"Mommy!" he screamed, and my mother came running. "She stole my favorite record."

"I didn't steal it. I borrowed it."

"You'll scratch it, I know. You always do," he cried like a typical sissy.

"Shelly, don't make Sunday more difficult than it already is." Marky's eyes dripped tears like a girl, and of course my mother hugged him. "Be a good sport, okay, pal? Your father is in the car already. He'll have a conniption if we don't get out there soon."

Marky dried his face with the backs of his hands, then smirked at me, the little creep, and skipped outside to the car.

Before I left the house, I went into my father's underwear drawer and took two quarters, a dime and a nickel which I would spend on a pack of Marlboro's the first chance I got. I took whatever I could whenever I got the chance. Retribution was my guiding principle. I got a thrill each time I got away with snatching something from one of my family members who I felt took so much away from me. In my brother's case, because of his "sensitive stomach," and buckteeth, he automatically became my mother's favorite child. I hated him for that.

Marky and I sat as far away from each other as possible in our own corners of the back seat. Leaning on the armrest, I flipped the ashtray cover up and down while staring out the window at passing shops, telephone polls, billboards and stop signs, the colorless backdrop of my childhood in West Los Angeles.

"Crook," Marky whispered.

"Selfish bastard," I whispered back.

"How are you kids back there?" my mother asked, sounding cheerful. "Isn't this fun, all of us together on such a gorgeous day? Let's just sit back and enjoy the beautiful scenery."

Riding around in the Oldsmobile with these weirdos was like being in a spaceship with Martians. "Who are these people?" I often asked myself, especially when we were confined in tight quarters, and I was anticipating my father's next outburst. Sometimes I couldn't help wondering if I was adopted, even though I looked like everyone in my family.

"Oh look!" My mother clapped her hands together as we approached the Pacific Coast highway and glimpsed the foamy white caps crashing on the sand. "Isn't it beautiful? Look, Irv. The ocean is so soothing. It's just what you need. We're lucky, kids. Children who grow up in the Midwest don't see the ocean until they're adults. Right, honey?"

"You bet your life they don't. Kids in California are spoiled rotten."

"Irv," my mother said, "Try to relax," and she touched his shoulder. "It's Sunday."

"I am relaxed," he said, gripping the steering wheel and applying pressure to the gas pedal.

I looked over at my prissy little brother. "Give me some gum," I said, and pinched his skinny arm.

"Ouch!" he shouted. "I don't have any left."

"Liar. I know you have a whole pack." I couldn't help myself. "Bugs Bunny," I yelled. "Everyday your teeth get bigger and uglier!"

"Okay. That's it. I've had it with you." My father swung his head around so he couldn't even see where he was driving and tried to whack me in the head. I ducked so he barely grazed my shoulder.

"I didn't do anything!" I shouted. Then I sank deeper into the corner of the back seat, out of his reach.

"Irv, for God's sake. Watch the road. You don't want to have an accident."

My father pushed his foot down harder on the gas pedal and I eyed the speedometer as it climbed from sixty to eighty.

"You're scaring the kids." My mother's voice strained, pleading for our safety.

"I'm just watching the road, Rachel. For Christ's sake! You people! Twelve goddamned Hoovers stolen out from under me by a bunch of crazy hoodlums. I could have walked in on them and been shot in the heart. You'd think my own family would give me a little consideration! It's fine for me to make the money but nobody gives a damn whether I live or die." Then he pressed the pedal to the floor. None of us could breathe. "To hell with everything!"

"We care, Irv, of course we do!" my mother shouted frantically. "Kids, please, no more fighting. Let's all get along." In that moment, all pending grievances between the three of us were suspended as we knitted together in obedient silence to keep my father from driving us off the steep cliff into the ocean. Even I clammed up out of fear.

All of a sudden, my father turned the wheel so hard that Marky and I were thrown together. We quickly untangled ourselves and returned to our corners, though we managed to give each other a horrified look acknowledging that we were in the hands of a maniac. My father burned rubber as he screeched through the Sea Lion parking lot, acting like he was on the run from the cops. Miraculously, he parked the car squarely between two white lines.

"Okay. Everybody out!" he said in a voice that suggested this particular parking spot had instantly restored his sanity.

"We're here," My mother smiled. Most people get in a good mood when something nice happens. My mother was encouraged whenever my father stopped acting nuts. She called it harmony. "Put on your sweaters, kids. It's cold at the ocean. Let's go have a nice, calm dinner."

"Lock the doors," my father said, checking his watch. "Right on time."

"Irv, how about a vodka gimlet? Might be good for you."

"I don't need it. But, maybe I'll have one," he said.

My mother looped her arm through his. I couldn't tell if it was a burst of affection on her part, or if she simply needed him as a crutch because of the woozy pills. I'll have a bourbon and ginger ale. That's what I like. The kids can have Shirley Temples."

"I want a Coke," I said. Shirley Temples were for sissies. Then, instead of walking straight ahead through the swinging glass doors of the restaurant, I veered away from my family, and made a mad dash for the cliffs, out to where the ocean crashed loudly against the rocks.

I stepped as close to the edge as I could get and let the wind and the ocean spray hit me from all sides. The fresh salty air and pounding waves washed away a layer of terror I'd felt on the drive.

Out on the rocks was a pack of sea lions, flapping their flippers and barking their heads off. They were beautiful, with slick dark fur, kind eyes and funny whiskers. Compared to my family they seemed so carefree and happy. It sounded like they were laughing, sharing one joke after the other. I watched them wobble along from place to place, scooting in and out of the water on their bellies; everything they did seemed like play.

On one small rock, I spotted a pup nuzzling up to its mother, the two of them bumping each other's noses and barking away. They reminded me of a time when I was maybe seven or eight, and Marky was just a little guy who followed me everywhere. One day, Mom decided to teach us how the Eskimos kiss. We all giggled because it tickled when we rubbed noses. I remembered thinking how beautiful my mother's soft brown eyes looked when she was having fun and how cute my brother was with his thick brown curls and innocent grin. We stuck close together just like the sea lions. Now we could barely stand to be around each other.

Sitting next to the pup and its mother was a large sea lion with giant whiskers, probably the father, who slapped his tail against the rock, and barked loudest of all, letting everyone know he was the dad. They were a happy sea lion family, huddled together on their family rock. That's where I belonged, with nothing but ocean all around me, swimming along with the sea lions.

Suddenly, my father clenched my wrist. "What in the hell do you think you are doing out here? Do you want to get yourself killed? Don't you think I've had enough aggravation for one week?" He was hurting me, so I said, "I'm coming."

My mother yelled to us. "Come on, Irv, Shelly. They just called our name." I followed my father into the restaurant, the only thing I could do, though I lagged behind, pretending that I wasn't his child.

"Nice to see you, Marge." My father turned on his charm for the hostess. He was good at impressing people he hardly knew. "Any chance of a window seat?" We got one in less than five minutes. "See, it pays to ask," he said, thrilled with himself. He hiked up his slacks, and strutted to the table ahead of the rest of us.

"Don't wander off like that again, Shelly, okay?" my mother said. "You see what it does to him."

"That's nuts, Mom," I argued. "He's been like this since before I was born, and you know it."

She opened her mouth to speak, then changed her mind, and gave me a gentle shove towards the table.

When the waitress arrived, my father ordered his vodka gimlet, Mom her bourbon and ginger ale, and Marky a Shirley Temple with a cherry. That fag. I ordered a Coke. When the drinks arrived, my father took a sip of his gimlet and smacked his lips. "Not bad, not bad at all," he said, settling into the cushy red leather booth, his arm wrapped around my mother's shoulder.

I inspected the crowd of customers coming and going. Most of the fathers smoked cigarettes and looked restless, as though they'd rather be bowling than eating with their families. The mothers seemed pale and worn out, chasing their kids up and down the aisles. Everyone looked like they'd been gypped by life, like they'd put a lot more into it than they were getting back. No one looked like they were having as much fun as the sea lions; maybe people weren't meant to be that happy.

The waitress returned with her pad and pencil and even though she smiled in a friendly way, she seemed in a hurry to get our orders and move on. My father gazed up at her. "We like to come out here just about every Sunday. It's the only day I take off from my business."

"Is that right? What can I get you?" she asked, pencil poised over her pad. Marky and I kicked each other under the table, and covered our mouths to keep from laughing. "I want a hamburger," I spoke up before my father could order for me. I looked over at my Mom.

She touched my father's arm. "Let her order what she wants."

"I think a Shrimp Louie is everyone's best bet. If you come to a fish restaurant, it makes sense to eat fish."

Just then my father's friend Mort from the Lion's Club sauntered over to say hello and the waitress said, "I'll come back."

"Don't get up," Mort said to my father who had begun to rise. "Jeez, Irv, heard about the Hoovers. Hell of a thing!"

"Well, watcha gonna do?" My father said and shrugged.

"Can you believe this husband of yours?" Mort said to my mother. "He doesn't deserve such rotten luck. The most generous and understanding guy at the club," Mort affectionately slapped my father on the back. "Anyway, thank god you're okay. Still, hell of a thing!" My father's face softened in a way I'd never seen before.

"Thanks, Mort," my father blushed. "Appreciate it."

"A mensch," my father said after Mort walked back to his table.

When the waitress returned, everyone else ordered Shrimp Louie and I ordered my hamburger and fries with no arguments from my father.

"I got robbed this week," he told the waitress, as if she were a relative. "Twelve Hoover vacuum cleaners ... out from under me in broad daylight. I could have been killed. Great to be out here at the ocean today where I can take my mind off things." The waitress nodded and walked away.

"Bitch," he muttered, and polished off his gimlet.

"She didn't do anything to you, Irv." My mother said. "So leave her alone. And leave the kids alone, too. Stop picking on everyone." It was a rare moment. Then she reached into her purse, and I watched her rummage around inside. Sometimes I worried she'd take too many pills and overdose like Marilyn Monroe. But she just pulled out her Orange Bliss Lipstick and ran it across her lips.

The sourdough bread and butter arrived, but neither Marky nor I touched it. Marky looked pale and scared and I wondered if he was about to throw up. My mother leaned over and brushed the bangs out of his eyes. She constantly played with his hair. How did she expect him to act like a real boy with her always coddling him?

"Look what you're doing to your son?" she said to my father.

"He's fine. Don't baby him so much," my father said, and continued his rant. "Where in the hell is our food already? Can you believe this?" he said to nobody in particular.

"I'm sure it's on its way, Irving! Relax! Look at the ocean, look at the waves! Look at the sea lions. Look at us!" My father ignored her and raised his voice so that people at nearby tables turned their heads. "This is no way to treat a regular customer!"

My mother looked embarrassed. Her eyes got blurry as if they didn't want to focus on anything anymore.

"Get the manager!" my father yelled, oblivious to our humiliation.

Just then the waitress arrived, her pale skinny arms laden with platters of food. "Here you go folks, sorry for the wait," she said.

"Damn right," my father said.

"We are slammed today, Sir," the waitress said, acting professional by not telling him to go to hell.

"Hold your horses," he said, and grabbed the waitress's arm. "Bring us some extra Louie dressing."

"Irv," my mother suddenly shouted. "Enough is enough!" Then she turned to the waitress and in a softer tone said, "So sorry about that. He had a difficult week." Their eyes locked and the waitress gave my mother the kind of look that said, I understand exactly what you're up against, before she walked away.

"Don't ever embarrass me like that again, Rachel," my father said. "You have no idea what you are talking about so just stay out of it."

"Go to hell, Irving. You just go to hell." The words flew swiftly out of my mother's mouth like poisoned arrows. Marky and I looked at her in shock. Was this our peacekeeping mother talking? She stood up and walked away from the table, wobbling a little down the aisle in the direction of the bathroom.

"Where in the hell does she think she's going?" My father asked, turning ghost white.

"To the bathroom," I said, and Marky jumped in, "Yeah, Daddy. To the bathroom. She's gotta go."

"Extra Louie dressing." The waitress swung by, sneered at my father and slammed the dish down. My father dumped the dressing on top of his salad, but it was obvious he'd lost all interest in eating. His eyes were riveted to the door to the ladies room.

Marky and I kept looking at each other as if he were each other's only gauge of what to do next. I took a few bites of my burger and Marky nibbled at his shrimp salad, but our hearts weren't in it, and I knew his stomach wasn't either. Mostly we sat there waiting. Five minutes, ten.

Then my father said, "Shelly, go see if your mother is all right." I went to the bathroom and looked in every stall but there was no sign of her. My heart pounded hard, as I thought about telling my father the bad news. Mom had never disappeared like this before. The farthest she'd gone was into the bedroom to "cool off." She'd close the door, draw the shades, put an ice pack on her head and come out several hours later, smiling serenely.

"She's gone," I told my father when I returned to the dining room.

"What do you mean, gone?" he said, leaping up from the table. "Where in the hell could she have gone?" Then he marched over to the hostess to report her disappearance.

"Marge, we can't find my wife." The hostess immediately assembled her crew of waiters to search for my mother as if she were a missing wallet.

"Stay here, kids," my father said when he returned to the table. "Don't go nowhere." It was the first time I'd seen him more scared than angry. He was sweating and pale as he took off through the front doors of the restaurant.

"Do you think she ran away?" Marky asked me, looking petrified.

"No. She's just trying to scare him," I said, hoping it was true. "Don't worry," I said, patting his arm.

We both looked out the window at the same moment and saw my mother standing out on the cliffs. My father was trying to pull her back from the edge.

"What are they doing?" Marky cried. "Is he going to hurt her?"

"No. They're just mad." I said, putting my arm around his shoulder. "Grown-ups do this. It'll be okay," I said believing it less and less. My father pulled on my mother's cardigan and it looked like he was going to rip it off her body. She pushed him away, then slapped him across the face. They both lost their balance and it seemed as if they might topple into the ocean. Then, they righted themselves and stood frozen glaring at each other. When my mother pointed her finger at my father like a pistol, I thought, If she had a gun, she'd shoot him. I wanted to run out there and stop anything worse from happening, but my legs were rubber and I couldn't move. Marky leaned into me and I held him close.

Slowly, my parents stepped away from the cliffs and followed the path back towards the restaurant, my mother walking ahead of my father.

"They're crazy," I said to Marky.

"At least they made up," he said. "It's okay now, right?"

"Yeah. I guess it's all over." I didn't tell him that I had a hunch that the worst was just beginning.

When my parents came inside, they both looked disheveled. My father seemed especially disoriented–all confidence drained from him–as if he'd glimpsed the possibility that my mother would leave him behind, choosing freedom over the safety net of his tumultuous love. My mother's hair was windblown, but her eyes were clear and bright. She looked young and strong.

"Are you kids okay?" She bent down to kiss the tops of our heads. We nodded affirmatively, wanting to make her happy and calm again. "You're good kids," she added, and I could tell that she meant both of us.

As soon as they were back in the booth, my father apologized for losing his temper. "I wasn't myself," was his explanation.

"The ocean really is something, isn't it?" he said to my mother after an awkward silence. She didn't answer him. Then he turned to Marky. "You know what I mean, Mark. The way it just keeps moving in and out no matter what else goes on? Pretty terrific, huh, son?" I realized that my father hardly ever spoke directly to my brother, and not once had I heard him call him, "son." Marky didn't say anything either. My father didn't dare look at me. So he turned his attention to the white water crashing on the cliffs.

"This is what makes it all worthwhile," he continued desperately, looking out to sea as if it might have answers for him. "Putting up with difficult customers and dealing with their crap is nothing compared to a Sunday drive along the coast and a delicious meal with my family." He was unstoppable. "Everyone makes mistakes, including me. You know, in the scheme of things, you got to look at it all philosophically," he said, twisting a napkin between his stubby grease-stained fingers, looking increasingly lost. "Learn to take things in stride. The truth is, it was only a bunch of lousy vacuum cleaners. Right? It's not as if one of you got sick or died, god forbid." He was all choked up now. "We're all still here together, which is what counts. You know you mean the world to me." He was so far gone.

The sun was beginning to drop, a giant red fireball sinking and melting into the sea. The water shimmered with silver flames, as if it were on fire too. I couldn't see the sea lions anymore. Maybe they had gone deep-sea fishing. Or maybe my parents had scared them away. The pounding waves hit the jagged rocks–pow, pow, pow–a reminder of the inherent violence of the sea.

My father reached out and touched my mother's hand. She pulled away from him, and reached for her glass of water. She didn't look drugged anymore. She looked wide-awake.

Mark and I reached for each other's hands under the table.

"What do you say we splurge and get hot fudge sundaes, celebrate how goddamned lucky we are!" My father's voice cracked, and then he started to cry.

My mother remained silent and unresponsive throughout his speech and breakdown, staring out to sea as if she saw things about our future none of us could yet imagine.

Fitbits & Fair Play

Louie's was a perfect shade of dark. Dark enough to feel hidden, but light enough for me to spot Mackenzie perched at the bar with her spiked platinum hair and delicate nose ring. When her silver blue eyes targeted mine, my heart started knocking. This is fucking crazy, Katy, I told myself. Why had I agreed to meet this hottie for drinks? My eyes swerved to the muscular curve of Mackenzie's shoulder where a Chinese tattoo symbolizing happiness resided in black ink, and I remembered why I'd come.

"Watcha drinking?" I asked stupidly, noting the muddled mint leaves floating in rum.

"Mojito. Weeknight. You know. Don't want to get too loaded." She laughed.

"Gotcha!" I said, and ordered Grey Goose straight up with a twist. "I'm off tomorrow," I explained, then settled in with my chilled martini, inhaling the stream of cigarette smoke drifting in from the outside patio. I swooned over the charbroiled aroma of greasy burgers wafting from the kitchen grill.

For the past three months, my girlfriend Emily and I had been on a strict abstinence program, kind of like Nazi camp for hedonists, giving up almost everything except broccoli. We hadn't had a drink or dined out in all that time. Now I was convulsing with desire.

Mackenzie must have sensed my hunger. "Want to split a burger?" she asked as I gulped my cocktail like lemonade.

"Why don't we each get our own," I said.

I ordered a Louie's bacon burger with mushrooms and a second cocktail to wash it all down. Mackenzie said, "What the hell," and ordered another mojito and a rare burger with Louie's secret sauce.

After devouring a few bites–both of us moaning with pleasure–she leaned forward and licked the juice dripping from my burger off my chin with vampire finesse.

"I've always wanted to do that," she said.

"Lick my chin?"

"No! Make the first move. I'm usually painfully shy."

Somehow I doubted this. In the next moment, gravity seemed to switch direction, forcing us to lean into each other until our lips hooked up in an off-center, sloppy kiss.

"I'm in a long term relationship, three years," I coughed up like a guilty child confessing to bed-wetting.

"I know that! I've seen you two together. She's cute. You're cute together. Three years. That's fucking amazing. I'm impressed."

Mackenzie was an intriguing girl.

"Louie's makes a great burger," was all I could come up with in response, given that I was experiencing an uncomfortable moment of déjà vu: The first time I had a Louie's burger was with Emily.

For the three years we'd been together, Emily and I had enjoyed an abundance of culinary pleasure and booze, along with crazy good sex. Occasionally, Emily talked about wanting to lose weight but was convinced she lacked the willpower to diet. It would be a challenge for anyone to cope with the glazed donuts that floated around her teachers' lounge. I thought her apple cheeks, framed by a gorgeous mane of Renaissance curls, made her more than sexy. She was voluptuous, but not fat, and I never hesitated to tell her so. As an artist and graphic designer, I have strong sensibilities regarding beauty. You could say my whole life revolves around truth and beauty, and, of course, love. Love is my number one priority.

It was at Sunday brunch over eggs Benedict and bloody marys, on one of those psychedelic fall days when the leaves are a riot of unreal reds and yellows that Emily shocked me with her declaration.

"This is my last indulgence," she said, patting her Rubenesque belly. "I'm fed up with being fat. Starting to-morrow, I'm going on a strict diet and cleaning up my act!"

Being intoxicated, I had chimed in, "I'll do it with you," even though I didn't have a weight issue or the inclination to clean up my act. To make it easier for her, I agreed not to drink. I signed up for Emily's health kick to demonstrate my commitment to her, offer moral support, and because she and I loved to do almost everything together.

"Awesome, Katy," she'd said, and we toasted to absti-nence with the dregs of our bloodies. We're both Libras and we'd been celebrating our twenty-seventh birthdays in style all weekend. Champagne, oysters, chocolate mousse. Bouncing from bar to bar to retrieve our free birthday cocktails. Emily had waited until Sunday to break the news because she didn't want to ruin one minute of our gastronomic fun. She's considerate that way. Emily is a doll.

To understand the temptations we were up against, you should know something about our little town. Here in Wellfax, our local health food store, The Great Earth, lies directly across the street from a string of retro bars where the well drinks are super-sized and dirt cheap. In Wellfax, wheat grass juicers coexist alongside martini devotees. There are fanatics on both sides of the street and there are always those who straddle the fence. I have always been more a straddler than a joiner, an independent caught between a desire for awakened purity and blissful oblivion. Essentially, I'd volunteered to give up everything on one side of the street.

The first week of self-inflicted boot camp, Emily and I bounced out of bed at daybreak, inhaled soy protein shakes, strapped on our Fitbits that record every step you take, every calorie you burn, and drove our Nissan Leaf to the nearby trailhead. During our long, uphill climbs on Mt. Tangent, we marveled at the staggering accumulation of "steps" and "miles," which eventually were registered as "badges" online, a techno-cool Girl Scout upgrade. One day, while chugging coconut water, we investigated the pros and cons of our endeavor.

"I miss my cocktails," I admitted, "but I'm not so fuzzy in the morning."

Emily concurred. "It's tough living without bagels with lox schmear, but finally, I'll lose this flab!" Then we both shouted at once, "Oh my God, we'll save so much money!"

By week two we'd begun joking about cheating.

"If I could eat anything?" Emily pondered. "Boca Nova warm chocolate bread pudding with a scoop of vanilla ice cream on top. How about you, Katy?"

"Grey Goose straight up with a twist. Maybe a double," I said, and we laughed. An avalanche of insights about the perversity of human nature occurred to us on the bumpy road to purity, as we grew more serious about our mission. Our spirits levitated above the town and we looked down on our former pedestrian needs and desires with a keen sense of our personal self-care evolution.

With systematic ardor, Emily researched our low-cal, healthy meal choices. We shopped with Gwyneth Paltrow sensibility, chopped and juiced with the precision of an Iron Chef. Our nighttime entertainment was dressing up an organic Rosie chicken with locally grown herbs, accompanied by steamy towers of leafy greens and filtered water, a Netflix movie and Mighty Leaf mint tea. We were in the eco stream. A super green, sustainable, low impact, fair trade, slow food, non-GMO, 100% pure organic Wellfax couple.

There was just one problem. After a month, we were living like lesbian monks. Nothing about our menus and daily workouts was sexy. Sexy was a margarita rimmed with salt, sexy was a juicy cheeseburger sloppy with mayo and catsup accompanied by truffle fries, topped off with a hot fudge sundae oozing whipped cream. Sexy was Mackenzie, sitting beside me now at Louie's ordering her third mojito.

By week five, Emily's boot camp felt like jail to me. The sky hovered like a forlorn gray blanket, threatening rain. The atmosphere of deprivation felt heavy and unrelenting. Though I was firming up, and my head was hyper-clear, rebellion gnawed at me like a rat. I was tempted to shout, "Enough!" but it felt like pushing someone off her zafu in the middle of a deep meditation. We had arrived at a great divide. I wanted more while Emily wanted less and less. She started cutting our portions in half, creating micro-puny meals to accelerate her weight loss. When I lost five pounds myself, and dropped below a hundred pounds, I insisted on taking seconds to avoid looking anorexic. She continued to eliminate items from our shopping list: gluten, cow's milk, nightshades, bananas and radiated fish. She lost seven pounds while morphing into a drill sergeant. I dreamt that I was behind bars, waiting for the zookeeper to throw me a steak.

Six weeks in, I ate all the leftover Halloween candy on my design company's reception desk. Miniature Snickers and Butterfingers meant nothing to me, so they didn't really count as cheating. My conscience was as clear as my blood alcohol level.

Meanwhile, Emily's libido transferred over to the gym, where she took endless yoga and Pilates classes, lifted weights and rode the elliptical. She weighed herself and checked her Fitbit scores several times a day, celebrating each calculated victory with a carrot stick. I cheered, faking weight loss enthusiasm the way some people fake orgasms.

Lying in bed one night, Emily surrounded herself with ice packs and munched on celery stalks. While the rain pounded overhead, each of us on our iPads, I looked over to see her reading a Dr. Oz article on the glycemic index of yams vs. sweet potatoes. She was living on another planet. We hadn't made love in weeks, or was it months? We're too young to be practicing celibacy, I thought, deciding to break the spell. I reached over to touch her and she recoiled. Was this an anti-inflammatory diet, as in, unable to be aroused?

"Honey," she said, not looking at me. "I told my acupuncturist about the headaches I've been having after Bikram yoga, and she said this is a perfect time to do a three-week liver cleanse. Are you in?"

"No, thank you. I wouldn't recognize myself if I was any cleaner."

She didn't laugh. Her sense of humor had evaporated along with her sex drive. I'd seen other people in our town get stuck on one side of the street, but I never thought it would happen to Emily. I certainly wasn't going to let it happen to me. Fuck this shit. Tomorrow I'm going to Louie's for a martini. But the next day, my desire for oblivion receded as my longing for connection intensified. After work, I went directly home to help Emily plant daffodils and hyacinths.

After two months, Emily had gone down a size. She swept through her closet, trying on archived clothes that for years had been too tight to consider. She was totally psyched, almost mad with body reduction euphoria. Yet she was also uncharacteristically testy. She snapped at me over insignificant misdemeanors. "You forgot to recycle the Kombucha bottles," she barked as if I had set the house on fire. She berated me for leaving the front porch light on. "Not very ecological," she grimaced. Not my easygoing, bon vivant Emily.

"How long are you going to do this fucking thing?" I finally asked.

"Until I lose fifteen pounds," she said definitively. "And I don't want to do Thanksgiving, either. Way too tempting. But you can go," she said, meaning to our friend Amy's where we'd gone every year since we first hooked up. "No. I'm not going to leave you alone on Thanksgiving!" I said, even though Amy made the best chestnut stuffing and was practically a sommelier when it came to wine pairings. Instead, I settled for sharing a bland turkey breast and steamed string beans at home watching the DVR of the New York Macy's parade.

When Emily returned from the acupuncturist with a large canister of chalky white powder, I couldn't resist. "We should snort it and go clubbing in the City."

"You'll see," was all she said.

During the three weeks of her cleanse, her headaches got worse. She checked with her acupuncturist who assured her she was just detoxing and shouldn't worry. Not worry? Forget the headache. What about losing your entire personality?

We had arrived at the two-month plateau. Fitbit was spitting out badges: 15,000 steps, 25,000 steps; You're a champ, the website repeatedly told us. You've achieved the equivalent of walking across The Serengeti, 500 miles! Italy was next at 750 miles. Emily's dream was to make it across New Zealand, 990 miles, by New Year's.

"What will you do when you get there?" I asked. "Run with the Maoris?"

"Don't joke," she told me. "This is important to me."

On a drizzly Saturday afternoon in December, while Emily went to sell a batch of oversized clothes at Image

Exchange, a second-hand store nearby, I discovered an ancient doobie tucked away in my underwear drawer. I lit a match and took two deep drags, then one more for the hell of it. Sprawled on our bed, royally stoned, I ate my way through a box of stale rice crackers while listening to Regina Specter sing, "You're so young! You're so goddamned young!" I considered masturbating but fell asleep while staring at a barren maple tree outside the bedroom window.

When I awoke, I contemplated my misdeed. Smoking wasn't drinking. Still, I was beginning to sneak around and lie to Emily, which I vaguely sensed could demolish our relationship like the first loose rock in a canyon that starts an avalanche. Before Em returned home that day I brushed my teeth vigorously, then made myself a strong cup of Ethiopian coffee to mask my crime. But when she came in, she walked right past me, anxious to haul out her yoga mat and practice headstands, her latest natural intoxicant.

By now, I knew I could sneak a cocktail and get away with it. Emily wouldn't have noticed if I'd smeared oil paint on my face, but suddenly, drinking alone seemed like a lonely and unrewarding transgression. I liked getting high with Em, when we would play with the edges of reality together. I'd lost my best playmate. We were in danger of going from doing everything together to doing nothing together.

My heart hung suspended between the two sides of the street like a pale, forgotten moon. That night I reluctantly returned to sobriety, Netflix and a child's bedtime. The next morning I rejoined Emily's army on a steep seven-mile loop on Mt. Tangent. I dragged myself along, tempted to spit out something scary like "Our relationship isn't working," but I wasn't sure if I really felt that way. Maybe this was a low point like the recession, and we'd soon climb back up to prosperity.

In place of sex and drinking, I wandered the aisles of The Great Earth in pursuit of delectables that might substitute for pleasures I'd left behind. Occasionally I snuck a slice of pizza or a brownie, which I ate in the car before driving home. Not very satisfying, but at least I was saving Emily from high calorie temptations.

Late in December, she stepped on the scale and screamed. She'd lost thirteen of her fifteen pounds. "I haven't weighed this little since I was twelve." She giggled.

"Congrats." I hugged her, searching for the old spark. "Hey, now we can celebrate. You deserve it. Let's get wasted on margaritas at Santos!"

"You're funny," she said, and ruffled my hair. Then she waltzed into the bedroom to do squats.

The week between Christmas and New Years' Eve, Emily woke up with what felt like a knife in her throat and a vice on her head.

"Shit," she moaned. "I can't believe I'm sick. I've been so good! I haven't eaten sugar in three months! Not even a Tic Tac. Why did I have to get sick during my fucking vacation? All my colleagues have been partying like crazy and they're perfectly fine!"

"I know, baby. It sucks," I sympathized, and brought her a pot of Throat Coat tea. Secretly, I was pleased her Nazi tactics weren't foolproof. And being able to take care of her made me feel a little more tender, and hopeful about the possibility of getting close again.

"I'll go to The Great Earth and get ingredients to make you chicken soup," I said. "Then we'll watch old SNL reruns. Laughter is supposed to be an immune booster."

"You're the best, Katy. Can you get skinless, boneless breasts instead of the whole chicken?" she asked, then sneezed a dozen times.

While Emily lay in bed with a fever, I collided with Mackenzie for the first time. It was at the nut butter station at The Great Earth. With her LuLu Lemon pants and tank, her flawless glowing skin and intense silver blue eyes, she could have been an advertisement for a yoga retreat: She wasn't just wholesome, though. She had a bold Chinese tattoo on her shoulder and she was cool-looking with her platinum hair and dark roots showing. She was grinding up raw almond butter, and I stood beside her, waiting my turn. As she secured her lid, she introduced herself.

"I'm Mackenzie. I've seen you here so many times but we've never spoken." She gushed about her love for nut butters and told me about samples of macadamia nut butter in the raw food section. "Try it. You'll get hooked!" Then she licked her lips. I thanked her. As she walked away, I noticed two baguettes in her shopping basket. She wasn't gluten free! Not every healthy person was.

That night as I spread macadamia nut butter on fresh challah, I thought about how friendly and sexy Mackenzie was, how easy it would be to fall for her.

Emily interrupted my reverie. "Katy, you're cheating," she said through her red, stuffy nose. "We're only supposed to eat gluten-free bread."

"That's you. Not me, " I said. "You're the paleo. I only agreed not to drink. A lot of damn good gluten-free is doing you! You're the one who's sick!"

"That's mean," she pouted.

"Sorry," I said, then spread the rest of my macadamia nut butter on a second piece of challah and ate it in front of her to show I was my own person. As my therapist always reminds me, over-merging isn't healthy either.

The next time I ran into Mackenzie was during the February chill. Emily was in training for a 100-mile breast cancer bike marathon. She and I were acting more like roommates than lovers, coexisting but unable to find our way back to each other. At night we rolled to our own side of our king-sized bed, leaving enough room between us for a treadmill.

Mackenzie and I converged again outside The Great Earth. She was leaning against the wall smoking a cigarette, which surprised me. Then as I watched her blow thick smoke rings in the air, I thought smoking actually increased her sex appeal.

"Oh hi, Katy!" She smiled–she remembered my name–and put her beautiful soft warm yoga hand on my shoulder. Fabulous circulation, I thought. Her complexion was rosy even though we were in the dead of winter and most of us on both sides of the street were pale versions of ourselves.

We headed into the store and towards the juice bar. Mackenzie was craving a Pine Ridge smoothie. "What are you getting, Katy?" she asked.

"I was thinking about a martini" I joked.

"Sounds good to me. When?" she said. A pregnant moment hung in the air like the ball about to drop in Times Square. I thought about going home to watch "Portlandia," then holding down Emily's legs while she did 200 sit-ups. "Twiggy," as I now called her, had lost fourteen of her desired fifteen pounds and was looking forward to "maintenance." Maintenance! What the fuck was that? She hadn't mentioned goddamned maintenance when I agreed to this self-deprivation program.

"How about tonight? Louie's at 8 pm?" What in the hell was I doing?

"I'm down," she said and pinched my cheek. "See you there." She walked away with cinematic slow-motion fluidity in her hips. I sensed the wildness beneath the calm. I was in deep trouble.

I continued down the aisles in a hyper-kinetic semi-trance, checking off the items on Emily's shopping list as if accomplishing this domestic task would tame me. Then I went home to help Emily prepare a low-fat, low-carb, no-dairy, gluten-free, non-alcoholic one-star dinner. She was humming and sweeping the kitchen floor when I walked in with the groceries. Predictably, she was wearing her Fitbit. She wore it like a chastity belt from morning to night.

"Made it! Lost the last pound," she told me, gleaming. "Now I can eat berries and cantaloupe!"

"Fabulous," I said, and went to the bathroom to wash my face. Suddenly I felt dirty. Emily had achieved something. What had I done besides go underground? I was a nervous wreck. I needed a drink to get ready to go out for a drink. Of course this was insane. I wasn't drinking! Well, at least not at home with Emily. Not in the confines of our sacred relationship, which was about to be shattered if I didn't get a grip.

"Don't forget. "Girls" starts tonight," she said as we cleared the dinner dishes.

"What time?"

"Nine, like always," she said.

"I might not be home in time, " I answered as nonchalantly as possible.

"What?" She looked confused. "Where are you going?"

"Nancy from work is freaking out. Her boyfriend's been cheating on her and she doesn't know what to do. I told her I'd meet her at Constant Coffee at 8 to discuss her options."

"That's a no brainer. Leave the fucker."

"Yeah, really," I agreed.

"You're a good friend, Katy. I love you." And she went to take an Epsom salt bath.

What an asshole I am, I thought. This is crazy. Emily has been preoccupied but deep down she loves me! If I'd had Mackenzie's phone number I would have called to cancel.

"Love you too, baby!" I shouted to make sure she heard me over the running water. Then I headed out the door.

"What's Emily doing tonight?" Mackenzie asked as we finished off our drinks. She continued to express intense curiosity about my relationship while actively seducing me. What did this say about her moral code? Or mine?

How long had it been since I'd had sex? What had happened to my wild and carefree youth? The clock was ticking. In three years I'd be thirty, and then I'd start worrying about getting a better job, maybe have a couple of kids, and buy all kinds of useless insurance. Responsibilities would pile up, and then I'd get tired and decrepit until the final chapter blindsided me and I was confined in a nursing home. My grandparents were headed there now and they kept telling me, "Just yesterday we were kids like you." Twenty-seven! I was almost old.

"She's grading papers," I told Mackenzie, and leaned forward just to see what it felt like to cheat. Just a taste. I let my lips touch the soft pillow of Mackenzie's lips. She slid her tongue into my mouth and my whole body jumped like a fish.

"Wanna come over? My apartment is only two blocks away." She laughed and I laughed along with her, unsure of what I was laughing at but certain that if I kept it up for too long I'd start crying.

I insisted on paying for the drinks and the burgers. It made me feel temporarily better about myself. As we walked to her place, not touching, I looked up and down the street to see who if anyone saw us come out of the bar. This is what it feels like to cheat. A blanket of paranoia descends and the fear and thrill of cheating become bundled up as one thing.

Mackenzie's flat was on the third floor overlooking a gas station and an abandoned warehouse. She shared the funky apartment with two other girls and a guy who were conveniently in Bolinas doing 'shrooms. We plunked down on the bumpy couch and drank Madera wine that tasted like cough medicine. Mackenzie lit a cigarette in the semi-darkness and I watched the tip of it turn fiery red as she inhaled deeply. Then she took a slug of wine right out of the bottle. She wasn't the health nut she originally appeared to be. She even confessed that she'd never done yoga. She just liked wearing Lulu Lemon clothes.

Though I was disoriented, the moment was still all about heat and hormones. I could feel Mackenzie's hip pressing against my thigh and my heart sped up faster than when I climbed the steepest grades of Mt. Tangent with Emily. I stared at the gaping slit in Mackenzie's jeans just above the knee, and for an instant I believed I had never seen anything so sexy. Then she was all over me. It was hot. It was new. Mackenzie was new. Why is new so damn sexy? She kissed differently, smelled differently, tasted and moved differently than anyone I'd been with before. She called me sugar and ran her finger down my bare arm.

"You're in awesome shape," she whispered in her husky voice, and I felt a wave of gratitude for the Fitbit and the crazy regimen Emily and I had been on for months. It was exciting to be with Mackenzie, but I was also a little sick to my stomach. Emily, I was thinking. My sweet, 1000-calories-a-day Emily, home alone watching "Girls."

The first year we were together my dog Whistler got run over by a U-Haul and Emily helped me nurse him back to health. She lent me money to get through my last semester of art and design school. And when my mother was diagnosed with pancreatic cancer, she held me close every single night for the months before Mom died. And then she helped me write the eulogy. She was the best thing in my world and now, for a little new hot sex, I was about to betray her trust.

Mackenzie smashed her cigarette in the ashtray, then excused herself to the bathroom. I sat frozen on the couch watching tendrils of smoke rise from the ashes. When she returned she placed a bamboo tray on the coffee table. Neatly arranged on it were a syringe, a box of cotton balls, alcohol swabs, and a metal spoon. What is this, some kind of concentration game? I mused, and then it hit me. Oh fuck, you've got to be kidding. This was way over my "moderation" head.

"It makes sex so amazing," she said. "We'll be like angels flying." Mackenzie smiled mischievously. Like corpses, I thought. I had the chilling realization that I was with a complete stranger, and one that I was no longer attracted to.

While Mackenzie was wrapping a cord around her biceps, I blurted, "I really should get going. I'm actually pretty worried about Emily. She has a bladder infection and I should be taking care of her, you know."

"Hope I didn't freak you out."

"Don't worry about it." What could I say?

"We'll do it another time then," she said, letting the cord go limp. Then she lit another smoke. "Maybe Emily can come too when she's feeling better. This was fun, though. I mean I liked kissing you."

I had to get out of there.

"Thanks for the wine," I said, and grabbed my jacket. "See you at The Great Earth."

"Take care now." She smiled bravely. "And tell Emily to drink lots of water."

I ran home the way Billy Crystal ran toward Meg Ryan on New Year's Eve at the end of When Harry Met Sally. When I burst through the front door, I was delighted to see Emily sitting on the couch watching the ten o'clock news with an afghan around her shoulders.

She turned to look at me. "Are you okay? You look pale. What happened with Nancy?"

"Oh, she decided to kick him out. I convinced her she's too good to put up with that kind of shit."

"Bravo! A victory for the girls." Emily gave me thumbs up and motioned me over to the couch.

I sat down beside her and clicked off the remote. "Enough news for one day," I said and kissed her cheek, which was cool and smooth and smelled like lavender soap.

"Have you been drinking? She asked.

"It was too noisy at the coffee shop so we ended up back at Nancy's. She offered me a glass of rotten Madeira and I just thought she'd feel better if I drank with her."

"That's okay, baby. Nobody's perfect." I looked down at the floor and saw an empty bowl with sticky traces of ice cream at the bottom.

"What's this?" I asked.

"I ate a couple of spoonfuls of the Häagan Dazs we had leftover from our birthdays. I guess I was feeling a little lonely tonight."

"Why didn't you tell me?" I said.

"You weren't here."

"Oh, right. Anyway, I'm actually relieved that we're being totally honest. I mean I'm glad neither of us is perfect. It's been crazy trying to be. Don't you think we're too young to give up everything?"

"Yeah," she said, letting the afghan slip off her shoulders and fall to the floor, revealing her beautiful, unblemished white shoulder. "Not everything!"

I went into the kitchen and got the pint of ice cream and two spoons. Just like in the old days, we took turns slipping cold creamy spoonfuls of Vanilla Swiss Almond into each other's open mouths. Then we dropped our spoons and began to kiss.

Emily's smile was never more gorgeous then when she lowered me down on the couch that night, unzipped my jeans and slipped a hand in. Before I knew it we were naked and completely drunk on lust. It's amazing how new everything feels when you're in love.

Twenty Minutes

In twenty minutes you will be dead. You could have called your husband at work to tell him you love him, or your mother, or your best friend, but there is no way of knowing you have only twenty minutes left on this planet so you ignore the robins at your window and spend seven minutes madly searching through the cluttered drawers in your bedroom dresser for an emery board.

"Where the fuck is it?" you say out loud, as you rake through empty eyeglass cases, expired credit cards, Nordstrom receipts, stray buttons and keys to who knows what, thinking, I've got to get rid of all this crap. Make a clean sweep. You'd love to get back in bed and read the *New Yorker* cover to cover, but right now, your pinky nail is broken and ragged and driving you fucking nuts. You march from the bedroom to the bathroom, and there on the second shelf of the linen closet is the prize. You run the emery board back and forth across your jagged little nail until it is restored. Only then can you breathe properly. You let out a sigh of relief. Your nail is smooth and your nerves feel smoother too, like when your darling husband massages your aching shoulders at bedtime. Next emergency: you cannot work, cannot write without caffeine. You are a journalist, incapable of finishing 2,000 words on global warming for the *Times* without espresso.

The phone rings. You see that it is your best friend, Ms. Endlessly-Fit-and-Motivated Gayle, in search of a running partner. You don't pick up. You're not in the mood. You are in the mood for one thing only. A good cup of strong Italian coffee from Peet's, "the best cafe in town." Things will be better; things will be good after a double cappuccino. You throw on your sweats. You're fast on your feet. You're in shape. And in a hurry because without coffee, you won't be able to write with clarity and aplomb. Funny word. Aplomb. You know that if you write today you will feel more alive, sane, and prepared to reenter the world, this big bad warmed-up, cranked-up planet.

As you back out of your driveway, a junky car you've never seen comes barreling around the corner. You slam on the brakes just in time, and your car rocks like a boat. Your adrenalin skyrockets and your heart pounds like a series of strong slaps. You hardly need the coffee anymore, but you are on a rampage.

Down the road you go, like a rabbit, eye on the carrot. You pass Gayle in her Lulu Lemon jogging suit and see her waving and mouthing, "Call me, Shithead." Your cell rings. It is your mother, your biggest fan. She emailed your latest piece on the BP oil spill to all her friends. You will call her back after you get your joe. You didn't sleep well. Dreams of forest fires, trees exploding, men with masks directing you toward a wall of smoke. No way out.

Earth heating up faster than ever. After your coffee, after you write, you will take a long walk with your faithful corgi, Casper, in the first-growth redwoods to clear the cobwebs from your mind and recharge your optimism. Then you'll be fit for company.

At the cafe, familiar patrons you see every day smile and say good morning and you smile and say good morning back. Other than your husband and Gayle, you see them more than anyone in your life. You would recognize them anywhere and yet you don't know their names or anything about them.

You order your usual. A double medium dry cap with one sugar. Today you have it with half and half. What the hell? Life is short. You gulp part of it right away as if it were medicine. It is medicine. You plan to savor the rest at home while you write, Casper parked beside you, thumping his happy tail. The handsome barista says have a great day, bella. You too, Luca, you say, and think, what a nice guy.

You get in your car. Your mood is rising like the temperature at the pole. You feel electric yet focused. Ready to rock and roll. You will finish your piece on global warming today. Yes. Inspired ideas circulate in your head like freshly popped popcorn: Community based local organic everything. Time to dig our hands into the earth again. Less commuting. More bicycles. No GMOs. That's what everyone needs. A return to simple and slow.

Fully jacked on caffeine, heart racing double time, you sense that you will accomplish something of great merit in this cutting edge piece. It may be your best to date. Award-winning. Pushcart Prize good. Suddenly, you are in a fantastic mood.

You call your husband to tell him you love him. But you get his voice mail.

"Hi honey, it's me. On your way home, could you stop at Whole Foods and pick up a couple of fat, juicy, dry-aged rib eyes? Let's barbecue. Open up one of our beautiful French cabs? I'm in the mood to celebrate."

After you hang up, you turn on the engine. A pain shoots through your head like the jab of a dentist's drill, then quickly disappears. What the hell was that? There's a low buzzing, then an explosion like a glass bomb going off between your ears. You lean your head on the steering wheel and the lights go out. The half-cup of lukewarm espresso rests in the cup holder beside you.

Vegetables

Lin is shopping at Whole Foods with her husband Marty, a pediatrician at Children's Hospital. Marty pushes the cart. Lin picks out the vegetables. It's been three years since Lin Fong arrived from Shanghai with nothing but a satchel and a dream of finding love and prosperity in America.

"Let's get beets to go with the lamb chops. Seventy-nine cents a pound," Marty instructs his beautiful young wife, then glares at his watch.

Lin hesitates, holding a plastic bag open in her hand. "We have already at home, Marty."

"So what? Seventy-nine cents a pound, Lin. A steal. They won't go bad, for God's sake. Come on. Come on."

Lin hesitates, then drops two fat beets into the bag and puts it in the cart.

Moving down the aisle, the pair agrees on tomatoes, squash, and white corn. When they get to the greens, there's more trouble.

"I would like to get bok choy," Lin says.

Standing frozen before the bok choy, Marty twists his handsome face into something unrecognizable. "Shit, Lin. It has no flavor."

Lin stares tenderly at the pregnant bundles of bok choy, each one as precious as a long-lost relative. She looks at Marty's bloodshot eyes, aware that he is tired from working on the pediatric ward thirty-six hours in a row. He is especially distraught now because on his watch a young boy died when his brain exploded in the night. Earlier, when Marty reported the bad news to Lin, she said, "It is not your fault, Marty," hoping to stave off his rage.

"For God's sake, Lin. It was an aneurism. Of course it wasn't my fault."

Despite Marty's opposition, Lin cannot help repeating herself. "I would like to get," she says, riveted to the bok choy.

Marty looks at her, then at the bok choy. "How about a compromise? Let's get artichokes. Ninety-nine cents each. We both love artichokes." His twisted grin makes her stomach do angry acrobatics.

Lin squints at the artichokes until they go out of focus.

"Get them," Marty says, waving his finger at the clusters of pointed green leaves.

Lin observes the degree of distortion in his face, then selects two artichokes and drops them into a plastic bag. She builds a wall around herself and imagines that she is walking through the streets of her village back home and will soon arrive at her parents' front door.

A little farther down the aisle, Marty shrugs and lets out a big puff of air as if Lin's silence has defeated him. "Okay, get the damn bok choy. But, hurry the hell up."

At the checkout stand, Marty reaches into his wallet, plucks out a fifty and slaps it down on the counter. Lin watches the friendly female checker blink and twitch as if a small earthquake has occurred inside her head. Lin remembers a time when Marty was someone else entirely.

They met in early January, in line at the hospital cafeteria. Marty was still a resident and Lin had only been in America for three months. She worked across the street from Children's Hospital at her uncle Gerald Fong's flower shop. Most days, she brought a sack lunch to work because she was trying to save her wages to bring her parents over from China. But when she became unbearably lonely, she treated herself to something sweet and delicious at the hospital cafeteria.

When Marty first noticed Lin's pale skin and cascading shiny black hair, he asked his colleagues what they knew about this porcelain doll. Of all the Asian girls he had dated, none were as astonishingly beautiful and serene as Lin. What a far cry from his crude, loudmouthed Brooklyn mother. Marty learned that Lin was single, shy, and worked at Fong's Flower Shop. He was amazed that no one had scooped her up. The next time he saw her in the cafeteria, Marty introduced himself as they each selected items from the display case. Then he passed her a napkin filled with silverware. Lin greeted him by lowering her eyes. When they converged at the cash register, Marty pulled out his wallet and paid for her rice pudding.

"Welcome to America," he said, looking directly into her eyes. "My treat."

Lin had noticed him too, and the plastic nametag pinned to his bright white medical coat: Martin Mills, M.D. He had thick, curly European hair and intense blue eyes. So exotic, so handsome, she thought. And a doctor!

A few days later, Marty put on his best Italian sports jacket, and used extra-stiff bio-gel to control his unmanageable hair. Then he walked to the flower shop where he found Lin, her Uncle Gerald, and his daughter Charlene, arranging bouquets for a customer's wedding.

Smiling brightly, Marty asked, "How much for a dozen red roses, Lin?"

"Nineteen dollars, Doctor Mills." Lin's heart pounded hard against her small tender bones then sunk low in her belly. These must be for his girlfriend, she thought, as she watched him smooth out creased dollar bills on her palm. He had large, strong hands. Lin placed each bill like a sleeping baby in the cash register drawer. After she handed him the red bouquet wrapped in sheer pink tissue paper, he handed the roses back to her.

"Something is wrong, Doctor Mills?" Lin frowned, then laid the flowers on the counter for inspection.

"No, nothing is wrong, Lin." Marty's face lit up like a lantern. Then he held her tiny hands between his own, creating a warm intimate sandwich. "They're for you!" he laughed. Lin's laughter spilled into his and flooded the flower shop as she hugged the American Beauty roses to her breast. Uncle Gerald and Charlene stood nearby, studying the pleased and confident expression on the stranger's face, attempting to determine its level of sincerity.

Every morning during the first month of courting, on his way to the hospital, Marty delivered delicate French pastries to the flower shop. He quickly won the praises of Uncle Gerald, who devoured most of the treats himself. "He'll be a good provider," Uncle Gerald told Lin. But Charlene wouldn't touch the sweets. "This is the kind of crap that poisons your thinking and makes you fat and subservient," she told Lin, who smiled at her well-intentioned but foolish cousin. Just because Charlene had been in America five years longer than Lin, didn't mean she knew everything.

For months Marty talked to Lin about his dream of saving children's lives. One cold winter's night, while they sipped pink cosmopolitan drinks at a fancy South of Market bar, he spoke of cutting-edge technologies, and used poetic words like the islets of Langerhans, corpus callosum and mitochondrial DNA, words Lin didn't understand but which sounded lyrical and mysterious to her. "You're so easy to talk to, Lin," Marty slurred, then ordered another round of drinks. Eventually, Lin revealed her dream of bringing her parents to America. Marty leaned in close. "I just might be able to help you out."

On a cloudless Sunday afternoon in May, Marty surprised Lin with a picnic in Golden Gate Park. He brought a wicker basket filled with deli sandwiches and a bottle of champagne. He spread his blanket on the lawn in front of the Arboretum and popped the cork. After lunch, Marty got down on his knees and opened a small black velvet box. When Lin saw the shiny engagement ring, gratitude caught in her throat like a bone. Marty stood up to hug his future wife and saw that he had grass stains on the knees of his white pants.

"Shit," he blurted, swatting at his pants like they were covered with ants. Then he reconsidered. "Hell, this is nothing," he laughed. "Just a stupid pair of pants."

Lin held him tightly, thinking about how close she had come to marrying the scowling, pockmarked businessman her parents had chosen for her in Shanghai.

As her wedding day approached, Marty was on call every other night during his neonatal rotation, working under Dr. Alfred Jarvis, a paunchy attending physician with thick, intimidating eyebrows. Even though Marty told him about his upcoming wedding, Jarvis kept applying pressure. "Dr. Mills, your patient has cardiac arrhythmia. Give us your differential diagnosis by tomorrow morning."

"I don't know why that prick picks on me. His timing sucks," Marty told Lin.

"It is wrong." Lin concurred. "You are too good and he is too mean."

Marty told Lin his mother Marsha was flying out from New York to help with the wedding. "She's efficient but scary," he said. When the two women met, Marsha held her future daughter-in-law's face in her hands. "Don't worry, doll. I've got it handled."

"Thank you. Thank you, Mother Marsha," Lin said.

"She's a sweet, innocent kid," Marsha said privately to Marty in her cigarette voice.

"And I want her to stay that way," he told his mother, "so don't fill her head with a bunch of feminist crap." To Marty, it was Lin's receptivity that was the essence of her attractiveness. That's why he favored Asian women. They weren't testy and demanding like his mother, a real ball buster.

"Lin's the best thing that ever happened to you. Don't screw it up." Marsha said.

Uncle Gerald and Charlene attended the ceremony held at a local reform synagogue. A dinner followed at a Chinese restaurant where they devoured drunken crab and sweet and sour pork. Everyone was in a friendly mood, even sharp-tongued cousin Charlene. Lin was overwhelmed with happiness; tears swam in her eyes. Wrapping his arm around her bare shoulder, Marty announced to the wedding party that once he finished his residency, he and Lin would go on their honeymoon. "Hawaii, or wherever she wants." He laughed, turning to look into Lin's dark eyes. Then he kissed his bride and everyone clapped.

"What would I do without you," Marty whispered in the dark of night after their erotic lovemaking. "You are my safe harbor." At first they made love in the traditional way, but then Marty began to experiment, twisting her body this way and that. She surrendered to his every desire, and fell asleep at night thinking of special things she could do for him the next day: massage his tired feet, prepare a hearty fish soup, listen to his heartbreaking hospital stories.

One night, after a long hospital shift, Marty came home and plopped down in his overstuffed chair. "I could kill that fucking Jarvis. I don't know what he has against me," he told Lin. "Do you?"

"No, I do not, Marty," she answered. "You are such a devoted doctor. You save so many lives. He should be happy with you." Then she brought him his Coca-Cola and pretzels.

For hours, Marty buried his head in thick medical textbooks. Lin occupied herself folding laundry and chopping vegetables for dinner. Chopping relaxed her, gave her purpose. And, within minutes of chopping she was transported to her mother's kitchen in China with its small wood stove and crooked floor. A deep calm would come over her. Tonight she would scrub and chop several healing mushrooms: shitake, enoki, oyster and maitake along with garlic and greens to keep her husband healthy. While Marty pored over his notes, preparing for morning rounds, she moved about the house, quiet as a ghost, observing him from various angles: the beautiful, strong bones of his face; the dark, unruly black hair; and the high forehead, knitted from too much worry.

It was on a gloomy Saturday afternoon that the couple went to Office Depot. Marty asked a clerk for a special plug for his laptop. The clerk wasn't sure he had what Marty needed but went into the back room to check. Marty paced, then suddenly shouted at a nearby clerk, "Hey, can't you get someone out here who knows what the hell they're doing!" Lin touched his tight shoulder with short, feathery strokes, until the manager returned with the required part. Marty asked if they had any kind of training program for their employees? "Yes, sir, we do," the man answered, clearing his throat. Lin felt sorry for the embarrassed manager but understood Marty's frustration. If Marty were selling computer parts, he would have read the manual 100 times before waiting on a customer.

"Those idiots don't realize how lucky they are to have a goddamned job in this lousy economy," Marty said as he led her out of the store.

"You are right, Marty," Lin agreed.

"No one understands me like you do, Lin," he said and took her out for an ice cream cone.

Marty slept badly while preparing for his presentation on M. pneumoniae-associated encephalitis at Grand Rounds. He was now doing his pediatric rotation under Dr. Janet Randall, a stick of a woman with a tight bun and black glasses too large for her bony face. Though she was small, she had strict, punishing eyes that made people do whatever she asked. Marty told Lin that Randall made his mother look like a hippie flower child.

He paced the floor at night, mumbling complex medical terminology. When he came to bed, Lin could feel his anxiety rise in his body like a fire. Marty was worried that Randall would humiliate him in front of his colleagues. Lin understood the importance of saving face, though she wished Marty could find a way to be happy again.

One night he startled Lin when he slammed his neurology textbook on the coffee table. She could feel his frustration curl within inches of her own skin, then recede like the roaring surf as he walked out the front door. While he was gone, she extracted the imbedded green eyes sprouting from potatoes, then stripped the tough stalks of broccoli and carrots before dropping them into a steamy fish broth. She added special sweet and sour spices she had bought in Chinatown, hoping the aromas would please and soothe her husband.

When Marty did not return she sat down at the small wooden desk in the bedroom, a desk Marty inherited from his father but hardly ever used, and wrote her parents a long letter, telling them all the amazing things she was learning in her new country. She told them how hard her husband worked at the most famous Children's Hospital. How he transplanted a glass eyeball into the empty socket of a seven-year-old boy, then helped give a frail little girl a new heart. Such miracles, day after day! She didn't mention how angry Marty got at his medical books or at the doctors in command. Instead, she told her family how Marty would soon be able to send for them and they would all be reunited in America!

When Marty finally returned that night, he apologized for "losing it over neurology." Then he held her in his arms and whispered, "I don't deserve you." This was the real Marty, full of love and regret. It was the terrible stress of being a doctor that changed him into an unpredictable man. These were the hardest years, everyone said so. Once he finished his residency, he would be himself again.

One hot summer evening, Marty drank three Budweiser's in a row, and forgot all his troubles. Playful as a child he flopped onto the couch and patted the cushion beside him. "Come here my gorgeous sexy wife." Then he proceeded to describe his dream of one day opening a low-fee pediatric clinic. He would be chief-of-staff and Lin would be his number one assistant. Together they would help thousands of sick children get well. "We'll be famous, Lin. Who knows, maybe I'll even have my own TV show like Sanjay Gupta or Dr. Oz!" Then Marty laid his head in Lin's lap, allowing her to run her hands through his coarse black hair while singing him Chinese lullabies. Touching the furrows in his brow, she tried to smooth away his exhaustion and resurrect the peaceful man she had married.

"Of all fucking days," Marty muttered on a Tuesday morning when he turned the key in the ignition and the car wouldn't start. He was already in Randall's bad graces. Although he'd done well at Grand Rounds, she'd balled him out for changing a patient's medicine without informing her. And now, he was going to be late to morning rounds! He tried again, but the engine failed.

"Maybe if you call the AAA, Marty," Lin risked. He looked at her as if she were insane. Then he got out of the car and called road service on his cell. Lin stared at the clock radio. When Marty got back into the car, she retreated to the farthest corner of the passenger seat and stared out the window, waiting for the road service man to rescue them.

When they arrived at the hospital, Marty dropped Lin off at the flower shop without a word. She waited outside until the heavy thud of her heart slowed. Then she stepped inside and greeted her cousin and uncle with a forced smile. "Anything you want to tell me?" Charlene asked. "Just a little headache today," Lin said. "Soon will be gone." And she went to her station to cut flowers for the day's orders.

That night, bounding into the apartment, Marty announced that his luck had changed. Miraculously, Randall arrived at morning rounds after him. "She was impressed with my answers. I nailed it!" he shouted, and grabbed Lin around the waist, twirling her in the air. For the first time, she froze in his embrace.

"I know. I was an asshole this morning," he said. Then he kissed her forehead, neck and shoulders with light butterfly kisses. "Forgive me?" he asked. "Forgive me for being such a bad boy?"

"Oh Marty," she whispered. How could she resist such sincerity?

After they made love that night, Marty paying special attention to her pleasure, he announced that she could stop working at the flower shop. They would manage on his salary.

"But what will I do, Marty?" Lin asked, bewildered.

"Study English. Work in the garden. Learn new recipes! Whatever you want!"

"What about my family? Can they come now?"

"When I get through residency hell," he told her. "And soon we can try for a baby. Would you like that sweetheart?"

"Oh yes, Marty," she answered. "Very much."

"Our real life is just around the corner," he said, squeezing her to him. "You'll see. We'll make your parents grandparents!"

"You have to educate yourself, cousin," Charlene repeatedly told Lin, suggesting books, and TV shows Lin should watch to empower herself. Charlene introduced her to Google and Facebook and Twitter. When Marty worked nights, Charlene picked up Lin and they drove to the gym to work out. "Lin, this is my girlfriend, Sydney," she said one day, introducing Lin to a tall muscular blonde woman running on the treadmill.

"Don't tell my father about Sydney, Lin," Charlene whispered to her cousin. "His thinking is planted in the old country." Lin was not familiar with women loving each other but she could see that they were happy.

With Charlene and Sydney's encouragement, Lin built muscles using steel machines, hand weights, and large, colorful rubber bands. She went shopping at Nordstrom's Rack with them and bought discounted short skirts and fishnet stockings. Charlene convinced her to splurge on a pair of wick-a-way yoga pants at LuLu Lemon and running shoes on sale at The Foot Locker. "Now you are a modern woman," Charlene said, slapping her cousin on the back. "Sexy and strong."

At night, hungry ghosts of her ancestors visited Lin's dreams. They wandered aimlessly through smoke-filled alleyways, wailing in the darkness. When Lin awoke, her heart raced and her skin was damp. She reached out to Marty. "Bad dream," she said, pressing her tiny bones against his. "Go to sleep," Marty said, sleepily. "I'm on call tomorrow."

Marsha came to visit two years after the wedding, and brought a bottle of fine Scotch and a Cuisinart as anniversary presents. "This contraption will make life a hell of a lot easier, Lin. Not so much goddamn chopping!" But Lin loved chopping. It connected her to her roots and gave her special time to contemplate and digest all the new information she was gathering in America. She would use the Cuisinart while Marsha visited, but then she would put it in storage and return to her treasured knives.

During their courtship, Marty told Lin his father died of cancer, but now Marsha revealed the truth. "Marty's father was in and out of the nuthouse before he hung himself. I couldn't save him. No one could. I had to save myself. Whatever you do, Lin, hold onto a piece of your independence," she said and lit a Pall Mall, displacing its smoke skyward.

After Marsha returned to New York, Lin went to see *Faces* with Charlene and Sydney, an old movie by John Cassavetes. She was practicing being an independent woman. When she came home, Marty was in the kitchen drinking a beer. He got up and pushed Lin's body up against the refrigerator, his hands wrapped around her neck like a noose.

"I want you here when I get home."

"But sometimes I don't know when you will be here."

"Then call my fucking cell and I'll tell you!" he screamed before releasing her.

The more medicine Marty learned, the less he seemed to care about people. He had promised her so many things: A child. To bring her parents to America. They would become "built-in babysitters," Marty often joked. Was he lying about all these things? What if Marty was as crazy as his father?

After long troubling days at the hospital, and too many cocktails at night, Marty sometimes forced Lin to have painful anal sex with him. He told her it was the only way he could relax. Lin went far away in her mind while he cursed and pushed his body so far into hers that she felt as if she might break apart. Once, when he was particularly overcome by demons, he knocked her head against the backboard, while shouting obscenities. Afterward he wept, saying, "I don't know what got into me." Lin wept with him, but now it was only for her own injured, relocated soul.

Sometimes Lin thought about taking up Charlene and Sydney's offer to come stay with them for a few days, "to get a fresh perspective," they said. But Lin was afraid to leave Marty. What would he do when she returned? Unhappy ghosts invaded him, and his fury darted out unpredictably like the fangs of a snake. Often he would leave the house in the middle of the night and stay away for hours. Lin would wait in fear, wondering who he would be when he returned.

One day, while Lin visited Charlene and Uncle Gerald, Marty stomped into the flower shop filled with customers. "I knew I'd find you here," he yelled. Uncle Gerald went into the backroom and sat down on a crate. Charlene stepped between Lin and Marty. "So cousin, have you come to buy flowers for your wife?" Shoving a bunch of sunflowers into his arms, she brought her face right up to his. "Now, get the fuck out of my shop." With all eyes on him, Marty slipped outside, gripping the sunflowers so tightly his knuckles turned white.

"Time to get tough, cousin," Charlene warned Lin. "Strong inside and out. If you want to survive, you need more oxygen. A strict routine. Exercise will save you." Obediently, Lin began to work out three times a week at the gym with Charlene. She did biceps curls, chest presses, and leg lifts. She took yoga and learned to twist her body into unimaginable shapes: cat, cow, downward dog, cobra. She felt like an animal. She felt quietly ferocious.

One afternoon in the locker room, after their showers, Charlene noticed bruises on Lin's throat that she had hidden beneath her turtleneck. "You shouldn't take his shit anymore. Even if he does pay the bills." Charlene said. "You could have the prick arrested," Sydney added.

Arrested? Marty? Her husband? The man who saved babies and had rescued her from marrying the pockmarked businessman?

At home, Marty constantly ridiculed Charlene and Sydney's relationship. "They don't know what they're missing," he said one night, jutting his hips forward while holding a scotch in his hand. "I think Randall's a dyke, too. It must be an epidemic! Stay away from those perverts, Lin, or you'll catch it!" Then he made a spooky, goblin face and laughed wildly. Lin quietly backed out of the room.

When she finished her daily housework, Lin channel-surfed. She watched Susie Orman tell Oprah that women need to have their own money. Susan Sarandon, Diane Sawyer, and Michelle Obama spoke about global warming, universal health care, equal pay for women. These spokeswomen seemed as smart as men. Ellen danced around the stage in her black jeans and white tennis shoes; she was one of Charlene's favorites, and Lin could see why. She wasn't afraid to be herself; her happiness was overflowing and infectious. Lin absorbed information about carbon footprints, sexual predators, failed mortgages, and greedy billionaires who always wanted more money.

Late at night Lin wrote letters home to her parents. They would still be able to come to America, she said, though she no longer could imagine how that would happen. On prime time TV, she watched a group of young people transported to the jungle to see if they could survive, be popular, and win a million dollars. If Marty was passed out on the couch from too much Scotch, she watched reruns of Lucy playing tricks on Ricky or old AMC movies starring Spencer Tracy and Katherine Hepburn. Katherine and Lucy were not afraid to fight with their husbands, keep secrets or even slam doors in their faces.

On a Saturday afternoon when Marty was working, Lin accompanied Charlene to her book group. Seven women sat in a circle, discussing a short story collection by an Indian writer while drinking chilled white wine. Although Lin hadn't read *The Interpreter of Maladies*, she enjoyed the friendly company. She liked listening to the women's passionate opinions about each story's meaning.

"How's the maniac treating you?" Sydney asked Lin.

"He was so good in the beginning," she said, after wiping tears from her cheeks. "I didn't know." As Lin cried, the women surrounded her and offered advice. They tried to convince her that she had done nothing wrong and deserved a slice of the happiness pie.

That night Lin dreamed she and Marty were standing in a field of overgrown grass. Sick children with helium balloon heads floated several feet off the ground. Marty grabbed at their ankles but despite his efforts to bring them down to earth, they floated back up into space. Lin watched Marty stumble and disappear into the tall grass. She reached out and pricked one of the children's helium heads with a pin. Blood, not air, gushed out and splattered her white linen dress. Lin woke in a panic, her heart banging against her thin bones. She was alone in bed. Marty was on call, she realized. She got up to shower. All that day she thought about blood pouring out of balloons.

Now Lin slices carrots on the diagonal, celery straight up and down. She dices onions and cries. She thinks about Marty's crazy fingers examining children's eyes, ears, tongues and reflexes. Are these children afraid of him too? After dinner she will leave him alone in the living room to unwind with the news. Though she misses her family terribly, she is grateful they have not arrived. Just as she is grateful there is not a baby growing in her belly.

She peels the tough skin of a beet, and its dark juice bleeds onto her fingers. She has a hard time slicing the swollen purple root. The knife needs sharpening. Usually Marty does this, but today Lin refuses to ask him. They haven't spoken since they returned from Whole Foods. Marty talked on the phone and she heard him say, "Oh crap!" Lin suspects that another child has died at the hospital, but she is unwilling to find out. Ever since they returned home, Marty has been yelling at the TV while cracking walnuts and chain-smoking. He smokes and drinks and occasionally swears at Dr. Randall as if she were in the room with him. Right now Lin can hear him dropping ice cubes into his scotch.

Lin looks at the raw meat on the counter and imagines it rotting. Suddenly it sickens her. Reminds her of everything that has gone wrong. She puts the lamb in the garbage and prepares her knife for fine slicing. She moves the blade back and forth against the long steel whetstone until bright light flies out from the shaft. It reminds her of the Fourth of July, three years before, her first in America, when there was still a bright light in her new husband's eyes, and his hands moved over her body like a gentle wind.

Lin places a bowl of vegetable soup and a plate of steamed artichokes and beets on the TV tray in front of him. For herself she has prepared a separate bowl of bok choy.

"What is this? Where are my lamb chops?"

"I forgot," she says coolly, and sits in a chair nearby. There is a dark screen between her and the world and it is steadily thickening like a cataract. She spreads a cloth napkin across her lap, then lifts tender stalks of bok choy onto her fork.

"What do you mean you forgot?" Marty looks shocked. His eyes become slits like her own.

"I cooked the vegetables we bought at Whole Foods, Marty. The ones that you picked out. Your beets. Your artichokes. Exactly what you wanted. Your favorite vegetables! All chopped up fresh and delicious."

"You idiot, don't be sarcastic with me. I work my ass off for you."

"For me, Marty?" She asks, arching her eyebrows. "For me and my family? And our baby? Everything is for us?"

"That's not what we're talking about. I'm not a fucking vegetarian. I wanted lamb chops, is that too much to ask, goddamn it?" Marty shrieks, as his arm swings around and catches her cheek. A blush appears, and slowly, as in a slow-motion film, Lin brings her hand to her cheek to cover the hot pain. She rises from the chair, drops the napkin on the floor, and disappears into the kitchen. Her heart is beating faster than a hummingbird's.

Marty watches her walk away from him and as he rises, he feels a weakness in his knees. What has happened to his adoring wife? Charlene has stolen her innocence. America has corrupted her gentle nature. I have simply tried to make a better life for her, he thinks.

"Honey, I'm sorry, baby," Marty says, as he follows her into the kitchen, feeling unexpectedly timid. "It's stress, that's all. I'm fucking overworked. So many kids are sick and dying. You know how I am. It gets under my skin. Listen, as soon as I pass the boards, we'll go away. Anywhere you want. You'll see. How about we finally go to Hawaii? Shit, Tahiti if you want. You know I love you, baby. It will be like it was. I promise. What do you say, sweetheart? Of course, we're going to bring your parents over! How about the moment we get back from Tahiti? Then we can start trying for a baby. Don't think I've forgotten our dream."

Lin stands at the sink, holding the steel knife in front of her, turning it slowly in the funneled light pouring through the window. She slices through shadows on the kitchen wall and fractures the rays of the setting sun.

Marty comes closer, straining for forgiveness. His shadow broadens as he approaches and fills the space in front of her. She can barely hear the muffled words he is uttering, but as she revolves, she can see that his mouth is working extra hard.

Her husband's face is as handsome as it ever gets: smooth, open, and radiant with desire for his bride of three years. Lin's mind is empty; her hands blossom with rage. A thousand female ancestors cluster nearby, whispering.

Flushed with color, Marty walks toward Lin to embrace her. She stands firm, ready to receive him.

Intrusions

One day Fred, my faithful husband of seventeen years, installed skylights in our living room and the next morning he keeled over in his oatmeal and died. Not since my father's murder when I was eleven had I been so disoriented. Fred was barely forty-two when he suffered his fatal heart attack, leaving me a widow at thirty-nine. Gerald, our only son, had just turned fifteen. Luckily I was left with the duplex, a charming Spanish stucco crowned by a red, hollow-tiled roof just blocks from the ocean.

For years Fred and I rented out the bottom flat of our Santa Monica home to a low-impact Buddhist monk who spent his days meditating and his nights cooking exotic vegetables in pungent oils. Intermittently he rang a gong. Beneath the monk was a basement where Fred used to tinker. I can still see his wrenches and screwdrivers neatly lined up on the back wall of his workbench, and the light in his eye whenever I'd tiptoe downstairs to surprise him with home-baked sugar cookies.

When Fred died, I refused to wither away in grief. I believe that women should pursue their own lives beyond tragedy. My practical mother had taught me this lesson when Daddy died and she continued to work full-time as a dental hygienist. In kind, I packed up Fred's belongings and phoned Goodwill. Then I converted his workshop into a therapy office.

For fifteen years, I'd worked as a psychotherapist at the Institute for Aging downtown, and I was sick of commuting. I was also sick of old people. I wanted to work with a younger, more optimistic population. I quit my job in order to start a private practice in the basement.

Gerald, handy like his father, helped me sheetrock, lay down a bamboo floor and roll out two coats of white paint. Before hanging my shingle, he and I carted in a couch, a chair, and a pole lamp purchased at Ikea. Too much furniture clutters a patient's mind.

After Gerald left for college, I treated myself to a conference on sexuality at the University of Arizona. It was my third year as a widow and none of my Match. com dates had led to the bedroom. Sometimes the loneliness was intolerable, and I found myself devouring whole plates of cookies still warm from the oven. I went to the conference to receive Continuing Ed. hours, but also to find a lover. Unfortunately, the few male attendees were plagued by impotence.

After the conference, refusing to wallow in disappointment, I took a bus tour of the Grand Canyon. A tall, lean stranger came down the aisle and asked if he could sit beside me. He told me he was traveling the Southwest, visiting his favorite rocks and succulents. He had taken an early retirement from his position as a botanist at the university, because, as he put it, "life is short and I want to have some fun." Hal's bright smile and unabashed friend-liness caught me off guard. He had beautiful white teeth. "Sure." I squeezed my body into the corner of the seat, making room for him. "Sit down, sit down. Please." He sat so close our arms and thighs grazed each other. Although he had greying temples and wore bifocals, I couldn't deny the chemistry. As it turned out, Hal was eighteen years older than me, but in remarkably good shape. And clearly he maintained good dental hygiene.

"You have beautiful eyes," he said as the bus bumped along the rim of the canyon. It's true. People have always said I have Elizabeth Taylor's eyes. Sadly, I also have her tendency to put on weight.

By the time we reached Death Valley, Hal had slipped his tanned arm around my shoulder and made light-hearted remarks about the bus driver's corny banter. Soon we were chattering comfortably about our impressions of the Red Rock Canyon and the Colorado River that snakes through it.

For over a year, not one of Hal's early morning erec-tions went to waste. What happiness! Each meal I pre-sented, Hal praised it as if I were a chef at a Michelin star restaurant. "Where did you learn to cook like this, Phyl?" Then he'd stretch his slim frame across the table to kiss me. The drought was over. I exulted in the warm, wet exchanges of deep, sensual love. When we made things more permanent, we agreed that $700 a month was a fair rent. The unexpected bonus was that Hal loved to work in the garden and fix things around the house. He wasn't Fred, but he was alive!

Gradually and cruelly over the months (who can ex-plain these mysterious shifts?), other interests–jogging, volleyball, men's things–began to tug at Hal. As his sport's muscles hardened, his penis slackened. There was always a tennis match on TV or a volleyball tournament at the rec center. I was often forced to watch Netflix by myself. The more I complained, the more he resisted. "Phyllis, I love you," he snapped one day, "but you've got to let me breathe."

I began to soothe myself with bagels and cream cheese for breakfast, and I put on a few extra pounds. Sometimes, I'd sneak off in the middle of the day to eat a cherry Danish on the seawall. To cover my expanding waistline, I wore loose fitting blouses and sweatshirts. I gained twenty pounds in less than six months, and went up two dress sizes. Hal added ikebana classes and sudoku puzzles to his daily routine.

Eight years after Fred's death, the monk gave notice and moved into a zendo. I had to find a new tenant. I decided a woman would be a refreshing change, someone who might become a friend.

I interviewed thirteen applicants, and selected Leslie, a tiny thing with short spiky hair. Though she was only in her mid-twenties, she seemed reasonably sane and sociable. As it turned out she was a fellow psychotherapist.

"My therapy office is underneath your bedroom, Leslie," I warned her. "Will that be a problem for you?"

"Not at all, Phyllis. In fact, I'd love to rent office space from you if you have any free days."

"As a matter of fact..." I answered. Due to crushing economic times, my client load had dwindled. Leslie could be my solution to the recession. "I was just thinking about renting the office."

"Wonderful," she said, and offered an additional $300 a month to avoid the commute downtown. "I know what that's like," I commiserated, aware of my power to release her from the bondage of the L.A. freeway! Three days for each of us, we easily agreed. Then, in a gesture of mutual appreciation, we hugged. A promising beginning.

Imagining the professional tête-à-têtes we'd be having, I kicked things off by inviting her upstairs for tea and Swedish cookies. Leslie arrived at my flat with an eager grin, bounding up the stairs as though she'd had several double espressos.

Her attention quickly went to Hal, who was hanging from his back inversion swing in the corner of the living room.

"That's Hal, my boyfriend," I explained as Leslie waved at Hal's upside-down physique.

"Looks like he keeps fit," Leslie said.

"Every morning he runs on the beach for an hour, rain or shine! Even though he's sixty-five, he sprints like a teenager. I spend my free time writing."

"That must be rewarding."

"Oh yes. I'm writing a book on women's sexuality."

"What kind?" Leslie laughed.

"All kinds," I said, matching her jocular tone.

Hal flipped upright. Looking trim as ever in a black T-shirt and khaki pants, his muscles like rocks, he strutted towards us. "Welcome aboard," he roared like the captain on 'The Love Boat.'

Leslie extended her hand. "Interesting contraption." She smiled flirtatiously.

"Stretches my spine. I've grown an inch."

"That's fantastic, Hal. I'd love to grow an inch!"

"By the way, Leslie," I interjected, "Would you like to hang a painting in the office?" -demonstrating I could be as welcoming as Hal.

"Thanks, Phyllis," she said. Her eyes remained glued to Hal's body.

"Do you like to garden?" Hal asked.

"Yes! The last place I lived had only enough room for three small clay pots on the deck. Drove us crazy."

Us? Had she just left her parents' home? Or was she in the midst of a divorce?

"You won't have that problem here." Hal said.

"Yes. I do have a rather large lot." I smiled and hooked my arm through Hal's to affirm our alliance.

"Fantastic. Karen will pitch in, too. She has a wonderful eye for landscaping."

Karen? Who the hell was she?

Hal unhooked from me and slapped Leslie's shoulder the way he slaps teammates after they score a point.

"Karen?" I asked just as she was leaving.

"My girlfriend," she said. "Remember, Phyllis? I told you I had a partner."

"Of course." I wasn't about to reveal I thought she was referring to her business partner during the interview. I pinched the acupuncture point for anxiety located on my earlobe.

"Her apartment and studio is in Laurel Canyon, but she'll probably stay over some weekends. If that's okay?"

"Of course it is!" Hal blurted as if he were the landlord.

Leslie moved in. I was just returning from the chiropractor when she cornered me in the driveway with an armload of paintings. She wore yoga pants and a snug tank top. One more athlete to contend with.

"Hi, Phyllis. I thought I'd take you up on your offer to put a painting in the office."

"Yes. Well. There is room for one painting over the patient's head."

"How about this one?" She held up an abstract yellow and red thing with giant flowers.

"Oh, did you do that?" It looked like a blindfolded three-year-old had painted it.

"No. Karen did." Her dark eyes were penetrating. "What do you think?" She touched my back as if the answer was lodged in my scapula.

"What else have you got?" I asked, struck by the immaturity of the work.

"There's this one." Her second choice was of an empty chair with an umbrella placed at the edge of a deserted beach: a desolate scene that could easily stimulate a patient's feelings of isolation.

"I'd been considering Renoir's Girl in a Swing, which I have stored in the attic. It's very soothing," I said. "We have to consider the patient's sensitivities."

"You don't think either of these are soothing?" She held up Karen's paintings again.

"I prefer the Renoir, actually, Leslie. But let me think about it."

Just then, Hal came along, sweaty from volleyball, wearing a skimpy pair of shorts and humming "On a Clear Day."

"Hey, Hal!" Leslie said. "You're looking taller!"

"How's it going, kiddo?" Hal bounced his ball a couple of times. "What a workout. Those college kids are going to kill me." He chuckled like a schoolboy. While he blotted his dripping forehead and chest with a towel, I noticed Leslie eyeing his flat abdomen. Hal smiled and shifted his feet like he needed to pee.

I had intended to invite Leslie up for tea and brownies, but I was losing my motivation. Perhaps she and Hal would prefer to hurl themselves into the ocean and swim with the sharks.

"What do you think of this, Hal?" Leslie pointed to the yellow and red painting.

"Ah! The deep reds remind me of New Mexico. A little of Georgia O'Keefe, am I right? Beautiful. Did you paint it?"

"No. Karen did." She beamed.

"We decided on the Renoir for the office, Hal," I said.

"Terrific," he said in that way he has of dismissing me. "See you, ladies. I'm off to make myself human again." He bounded upstairs to shower, never missing an opportunity to exhibit his stamina. Often, when Hal was beet red in the face after a brutal day on the courts, I imagined him suddenly collapsing like Fred.

One week after moving in, Leslie began to clutter the office with artsy-cutesy crap: a jagged crystal, embossed business cards on a redwood stand, and a scented candle that made me sneeze. In three years, the only extra thing I'd brought in was a brass coat rack. I try to give the patient a sense of object constancy. I realized I hadn't clarified the rules of sharing a professional space. In fact, I wondered if I had made a mistake letting Leslie in. She seemed so ... self-propelled.

When my most depressed patient, Rose, made a fuss over Leslie's Kleenex box decorated with butterflies, and remarked that the crystal gave her courage, I reconsidered asking Leslie to remove her knickknacks. I smiled at Rose and told her that I was glad my decorations lifted her spirits.

Next thing I knew, Leslie and another woman with long blonde hair were down on their knees in my garden. They had dragged rocks, shrubs, and trays full of pansies and zinnias from blondie's truck into the yard and were strategically arranging them in the earth.

"Hey, Phyllis." Leslie looked up, her face smeared with dirt. "This is Karen."

Karen raised a gardening glove in the air and smiled broadly. Slim and relatively pretty. Other than her blue Ford pickup, you'd never have guessed she was a lesbian.

"Very nice." I smiled, giving the garden a quick once over. Then I walked upstairs out of the dangerous afternoon rays.

She's certainly making herself at home," I said to Hal, as I gazed out the window, watching them shovel horse manure into my soil.

"Isn't it great? They both have a strong appreciation for nature. This morning they told me how much they love my prickly pears."

"I appreciate your prickly pears, Hal."

"I'm glad to hear that, Phyl." He put his arms around my waist, which made me self-conscious because of my recently acquired folds of fat. I wiggled away from his embrace and looked him in the eye.

"I like flowers, Hal, but Leslie acts like it's her garden. Next thing she'll be going to ikebana classes with you."

"I'd love the company," he said. "You never want to come."

"Well, I am trying to write my book, in case you've forgotten. I can't go to every class you sign up for."

"Fine," he said. "Write your damn book." Then he went about misting the indoor plants. That evening I rode Hal's stationary bike for twenty-two minutes, broke out in a sweat, and trembled for the rest of the night. I ate half a bag of Oreos and downed a glass of warm milk to calm my nerves. By the next morning, I was back on the chiropractor's table.

I knew Karen was around whenever I heard raucous conversation coming through the vents. Essentially she was poaching on my property. The extra utilities alone would cost me a fortune. I'd have no choice but to raise the rent. Sometimes the burden of being a landlady is overwhelming.

I mentioned the idea of a rent hike to Hal and he was against it. "Phyl," he said, "the effort Karen and Leslie make in the garden more than outweighs any additional energy costs."

"Well, every time they work in the garden they have to take a shower," I said. "Think about it."

During the next few months, I watched the three of them transform my garden into an arboretum adding more plants, rocks, a rose bush and an orange tree. They staked a trellis for tomatoes and twisted sweet pea vines around my fence, all the while sharing a million inside jokes; one or two code words sent them into hysterics. Concentrating on my writing was becoming impossible.

It wasn't long before Hal was climbing ladders to change light bulbs and install blinds in Leslie's flat. Screwing together a bookcase, assembling an earthquake preparedness kit, he seemed almost giddy about the added chores.

From my upstairs window, I'd listen to him and the girls discuss the health of their plants as if they were co-parenting children: Who liked direct sunlight? Who required shade? Who needed space? Who was thirsty? Who craved which fertilizers? Soon, they'll be taking the plants' temperatures and reading them bedtime stories, I thought, as they huddled together, whispering over a cactus. Karen was around more and more often.

"Giving pruning lessons, Hal?" I asked at breakfast one morning while we ate poached eggs and toast.

"What's bugging you, Phyl?" Hal slowly spooned the yolk into his mouth, swallowing it whole.

"Don't forget this is my house, Hal."

"Who could forget?"

"I could evict Leslie if I wanted to, since she snuck Karen in without my permission!"

"And what about the illegal office? No permits, remember? Don't get embroiled in something you can't get yourself out of, Phyllis. Besides, they're good kids!"

"If I'd known her girlfriend was moving in I never would have chosen Leslie."

"What if Karen had been Kevin?"

"You know I have gay friends."

"For instance?"

"Well, not friends exactly. But Marjorie's daughter is a lesbian."

"You haven't seen Marjorie in years."

"That's beside the point. We're still Facebook friends!"

A charged silence enveloped us as Hal slathered butter on his second piece of toast. The skinny bastard eats whatever he wants.

"What about the oversized Buddha head they schlepped in yesterday? What do they think this is? A monastery?" I laughed, but it came out sounding as if I was choking.

"If you don't like something they do, tell them. I'm sure they'll be cooperative." He sauntered across the room, poured himself a glass of filtered water. Hydration seemed to alter his mood. "Listen kiddo. Let's make a fresh start. Karen is staying over tonight and the girls invited us out for a drink at the new tapas bar in Venice. How about it? Let's have a little fun. Remember fun?"

"Tonight?"

"Yes!"

"It's the middle of the week, Hal. I should work on my book."

"Suit yourself. But I'm going." Hal went into the bathroom to shave, leaving his crust on the plate.

"I'll think about it," I yelled to him.

As I cleaned the dishes, I knocked over and broke one of his precious Hopi idols, an ugly little aborigine with feathers sticking out in every direction. I cleaned up the debris and threw the shattered pieces in the trash.

My heart banged in my ears. Unconsciously, I had eaten the remnants of Hal's toast. Why was he so intent on becoming friends with a pair of twenty-something homosexuals? The last place I needed to spend my adult life was in an unventilated gay bar with fattening appetizers. I'd have to sit and listen to Hal and the tenants discuss soil conditions and bug spray without an opportunity to utter a word about my book. Writers are so disregarded. Not until you get a rave review in the *New York Times* does anyone pay attention to the book you've slaved over for a decade. And, then, suddenly, you're famous and everyone wants to have lunch with you!

When Hal came in that night reeking of cigarettes and wine, I pretended to be asleep. I peeked at the clock. 1:47 a.m. I was glad I hadn't joined them in their debauchery!

The next day, I bumped into Leslie outside the office. "Celeste Beakman is going to be holding her grief group here on Saturdays," I told Leslie, even though I hadn't yet responded to Celeste's request to use my office.

"I didn't know you were renting the office to other people, Phyllis," she said.

"Actually we're doing a trade. In exchange for using the office, Celeste has offered to vacuum, dust, and keep things tidy. Won't that be nice for both of us? Celeste is one of my oldest patients."

Leslie narrowed her eyes. "You're renting the office to patients?"

"Saturday is my day," I said, and went upstairs to call Celeste. Lengthy explanations to tenants weaken a landlord's position; I had to be succinct if I was to maintain my footing.

Gerald, who was now a certified life coach, asked if he and a few of his buddies could hold their weekly poker game in the office during my Tuesday night slot. Why the hell not? After all, he helped me renovate the place. Like his father, he had always been on my side. As anticipated, Leslie and her sidekick arrived at my front door after Gerald's first game night, ready for combat.

"Phyllis! Who are these other people using the office? They leave beer cans and cigarette butts all over the place."

"Gerald is not 'other people,' Leslie. He's my son." I smiled to show I'd made my point. "Besides, none of Gerald's friends smoke."

"Well somebody's butts are in the potted ficus!" Leslie raised her voice.

"They stayed past midnight, Phyllis, and we could hear every word from our bedroom," Karen added.

Our bedroom! Ha!

"I did warn you when you took the flat, Leslie, that the office was under you. Excuse me, please. I have a conference call with my editor." I smiled and closed the door. Exhausted from the confrontation, I plopped down in my overstuffed armchair and fell asleep.

Rose, my depressive, returned from a vacation in Bermuda. "I've taken up snorkeling and rock climbing." She lit up. "And I've lost twenty-five pounds." Rose declared herself cured and quit therapy. I suspected she was in a manic phase and would be back. But I smiled encouragingly and wished her well. "Good for you, Rose. Call me if you have a relapse."

On Friday afternoon the threesome made plans to return to the bar.

"Wanna come?" Hal asked. "Tonight is half-price margaritas."

"Margaritas?" I didn't need the calories. "I'm sure Leslie and Karen don't want me there," I said, feeling especially vulnerable after a Rolfing session.

"No. They specifically asked for you, Phyl," he said. Was it possible they wanted to apologize?

"They did?"

"Yes!" Hal smiled invitingly.

"Well, I guess once couldn't hurt." I smiled back.

"That's the ticket!" Hal laughed, and for a moment I felt like we were in love again.

When we got to the bar, they all ordered top shelf margaritas so I got one too. I felt a little tipsy after a few sips, so I slowed it down, but they quickly ordered a second round. Pretty soon, they were all inebriated.

Out of the blue, Karen said, "Hey Phyllis, tell us about your book."

I was shocked at her interest and a little drunk myself. That's why I opened up and told them all about my interviews with women suffering from sexual rejection due to obesity. They listened politely but didn't comment. When I got home, I regretted sharing such sensitive material with strangers. The next day, I could hardly face any of them.

Gerald and I decided to co-lead a ten-week Mothers and Sons Communication Workshop on Sunday afternoons. I slipped a note under Leslie's door.

"You must be kidding! Sundays, Phyllis?" As I expected, Leslie arrived at my door, accompanied by her string bean shadow. Karen seemed to get narrower each time I saw her. Maybe she had an eating disorder.

"Half the Sundays are mine."

"You never said anything about Sundays."

"Well, now you know."

"Phyllis, we all need a day to relax," Karen said.

I looked directly into her eyes and said, "I don't remember renting to you."

"She's only here three nights a week!" Leslie's eyes were crazed, her fists clenched.

"Well, three times a week is too many," I rebutted. I was afraid Leslie was going to take a swing at me, so I backed up. Karen took Leslie's hand and they marched downstairs. Clearly, I had re-established my rightful authority. Even so, I felt faint. I sat in the overstuffed chair for a few minutes, taking deep breaths. Then I did a dozen kegels. I opened up the L.A. Times and scanned the headlines. Endless Mid-East conflict. Bombs going off everywhere. Teenage terrorists blowing themselves up. No wonder there's so much war; people can't stand each other. I got up, poured myself a glass of milk, and gnawed on the leg of lamb bone from the previous night's dinner.

After the porch incident, Leslie barely acknowledged me. Hal's garden friendship with the girls continued. In February, Leslie purchased a large flat-screen TV, and Mr. Endlessly Helpful installed it along with a Roku box. On Sunday nights, Hal tiptoed downstairs to watch Homeland and House of Cards with them. Needless to say, I was not invited to these popcorn fiestas.

"They hate me," I told Hal, "even though if it wasn't for me, they'd be homeless."

"That's quite an exaggeration, Phyllis. And besides, don't you think you should look at your part?"

"Meaning?"

Hal made a tent with his fingers and stared at me. "Honestly, Phyllis, you've never really made them feel welcome."

"Leslie's a sneak and Karen's a parasite. It is my house!" I shouted.

"We all know that," Hal shouted back. "We may be tenants, but we're people too."

"Whose side are you on?" I asked.

"I'm on the side of everyone getting along," he answered. He looked like he had more to say, but he tucked his basketball under his arm and escaped to the playground.

The very next day I saw him deliver one of his prize Japanese arrangements from Ikebana class to their front door. I couldn't help myself. "Why don't you move in downstairs?"

"Maybe I will," he said and walked away.

All summer, we ate our meals in silence and slept on opposite sides of the bed. I stared at his bony spine. Hal had become a stranger to me. I couldn't focus on my book for more than a few minutes. Recalling the quiet days of the monk with remorse, I started fantasizing about getting rid of all three of them.

One sweltering night in mid-August, I woke up to the piercing sounds of Leslie and Karen having sex. Hal was asleep. I bumped him. "Hal, they're at it again."

"They're just having a good time, Phyllis. Go back to sleep," he groaned. Then he rolled over and began to snore. Hal slept through everything. He was perfectly happy with the way things had turned out. He had his shelter, his volleyball, his garden, and his girls. What was I getting out of living in this ridiculous commune?

I lay there considering strategies to evict them. Maybe I would ask Gerald to move in. Having a relative on the property would ensure my safety and protection.

For over an hour, I reviewed each of their betrayals. A particularly piercing affront was that Hal had abandoned me every Sunday night to watch Homeland with those ingrates! How heartless he had become. I got up and poured a stiff shot of Hal's expensive brandy, downing it in one gulp. Then, I poured another. The brandy stung my throat but it was giving me courage like the crystal had given Rose.

Wearing only my thin cotton nightgown, brandy bottle in tow, I crept downstairs and outside to the garden. I looked up at the black sky, and loneliness stabbed me in the chest like a blunt knife. I took another swig. My knees buckled, and I found myself kneeling in the dirt, raking my fingers through the rich loamy soil. Insects scurried beneath my fingertips.

"This is my house! My garden–isn't it?" I asked the empty sky. Dizzy with despair, I began to yank up the annuals by the roots and toss them over the vine-covered garden fence. Pansies, zinnias, lobelia, all easy to remove; the bougainvillea was more stubborn, but I prevailed. The roses were a bitch. I fought to get a grip on the trunk of Hal's American Beauty, but I kept pricking my fingers on the thorns and scratching my palms and wrists. My hands were torn up and bleeding. Even though the rose bush refused to budge, I'd done major damage to the garden. When I finished, the yard looked as though a rhino had plowed through it.

My bare arms were covered with mud and blood. When I touched my face, it was damp with tears.

"Fucking tenants," I muttered, lying prone on the dirt. "Look what you've done to me." I could feel my pulse slapping against the earth. My body trembled, twitched and heaved until there was nothing left.

An unexpected calm came over me. In the darkness, I remembered lying beneath the family apple tree the year before my father was gunned down by thugs at his pawnshop. Puffy clouds drifted across a blue sky as my back sank into the soft green mattress of our backyard. I had known true happiness, before it was harshly ripped away from me.

Too exhausted to move, I inhaled the salty ocean air and listened to the crashing waves in the distance exquisitely collaborate with the hypnotic clicking of crickets. I lay perfectly still, absorbing the simple and perfect harmony of nature. Then I had a revelation. Why was I still trying to write a book I didn't give a shit about? Maybe there was something to what Hal was trying to tell me. Wasn't his easy-going, fun-loving nature what attracted me to him in the beginning, his deep appreciation of life's simple pleasures?

I thought back to our early carefree days together. The look of love in his eyes was undeniable, and the laughter we shared walking barefoot on the sand had made me feel young, beautiful, and free! Hal had loved me once. Was it possible we could reconcile and be happy again? Breathing in the intoxicating night air, a pure wave of optimism washed over me.

Then the ocean chill began to penetrate my bones. Shivering, I rose from the dirt, brushed myself off, and scurried upstairs. Half way up, I panicked. How would I explain my devastation of their Garden of Eden?

I ran back downstairs and dashed around to the other side of the fence where I'd thrown the plants. Lifting the skirt of my nightgown, I formed a basket to carry the mutilated flowers back into the garden. Meticulously, I returned each plant to what I guessed was its designated place. I tamped down the dirt around the crowns as I had seen Hal and the girls do. I removed several dead leaves and broken stems. Dragging the hose from the shed, I gave each plant a little squirt of water. Certainly, I had as much right as anyone to tend to my own garden!

I turned the hose up and washed all the dirt and blood from my arms, fingernails, and face. Vigorously, I brushed the filth from my nightgown, attempting to remove every speck of evidence against me. One more slug of brandy to warm up!

Then, empty bottle in hand, I tiptoed up the porch stairs to go inside and change out of my soiled nightgown. When I turned the knob, I was horrified to find that the door was locked. I trembled at the thought of knocking on my own door. How would I explain to Hal what I was doing outside in the middle of the night, half drunk?

Just then the downstairs light went on, flooding the garden.

"Who's out there?" I heard Karen say.

"Nobody baby," Leslie said. "Let's go back to bed."

I crouched in the doorway as they disappeared inside.

Grass Valley

The South Fork of the Yuba River flows through California's Mother Lode gold country in the foothills of the Sierra Nevada Mountains, ten miles outside of Grass Valley. We've timed our visit just right to watch the changing leaves perform a fluttery Sufi dance of liquidambar, maple and gingko in luminous reds, oranges and gold. Radiant swirls of light strike the windows of this cozy vacation rental while inside Jerie and I are sunk into recliners to drink coffee and write in Moleskine journals, two Yuba miners digging for gold, unfamiliar with the territory yet committed to the excavation. It isn't easy. Between us, we are lifting heavy boulders of grief. In the last three years, both Jerie's sons died in their forties, destroying the natural order of things–one generation at a time, elders first. Instead, it is Lane who is first, murdered in Mexico, and two years later, Reid, felled by a heart attack in our home. We have come here, not so much to get away from the unalterable truth as to create a place of silence and peace where they can come to us more easily and fully. When we're settled in the quiet of nature, they show up.

Along the banks just past the covered bridge, we can feel them with us. Reid in his baggy, bright yellow shorts and unlaced hiking boots, surfing the web on his iPhone, his soft brown eyes and disarming smile identical to his mother's. And Lane, with Jerie's contagious laughter and keen sense of direction, is our compass. You can't get lost if Lane is with you.

We carry snacks in cardboard containers purchased at the local deli, cautious not to trip on a loose rock or protruding tree root on the bumpy path. I can't resist removing my shoe and dipping my toe in.

"It's freezing!" I shout.

"Go in anyway." Jerie carries the grocery bag to the picnic table and smiles playfully–each moment of levity, an unexpected gift.

Sitting on picnic benches scarred by lovers' initials, we don't talk about Lane and Reid. We don't have to. They're present in the way the light cuts into boulders, the slow crawl of cold water across the river rocks, the fresh, spicy smell of moist earth. Finches and warblers fill the pines with songs that sound like hope to me, and the mountain air is exhilarating. I can't help taking full breaths and feeling a bit intoxicated. With the sun warming our faces, I set paper napkins and plastic forks on a heavily stained, redwood picnic table and pass the Greek salad, hummus and baguette. We eat in silence. It used to be unbearable to watch Jerie cry, but I've learned that breaking down is good medicine, and I try not to fix it.

"I'm amazed I haven't lost my mind," she says.

The last time we came here, we were in our early thirties, muscular and trim, we took turns diving from twenty-foot cliffs into the icy river below. We loved to shock ourselves back then.

"We were naked and half drunk the whole trip," Jerie remembers.

We slept under the stars in sleeping bags zipped together, unencumbered vagabonds newly in love. Night animals growled things we didn't yet understand–the dark, scary, unfathomable truth of how life changes in a moment. How love becomes not merely about giving and receiving pleasure, but a way of seeing each other through the twists and turns, a commitment to hold each other up.

Jerie thanks me for sticking it out all these years.

"You too," I say, taking her hand. "Where shall we go next?"

"How about Africa?" she says. "Let's go on a safari." In the picture in my mind, Lane navigates us across the wide savanna in a jeep while Reid rides behind on an elephant wearing a stylish floppy hat. With his high-tech binoculars, he scans the horizon for lions and tigers.

Amends

I've been around lesbians my entire life. In fact, my favorite Aunt Nikki is a dyke. She and her girlfriend Deborah have been together since I was in Pampers. That was twenty-three years ago, when it was a lot harder to be gay. I have giant respect for my aunts and the rough road they've traveled. Their generation made it so much easier for girls like me to take the leap.

When Francesca and I hooked up at a New Year's Eve party, Nikki and Deborah were the first two people I told, and two weeks later, they cooked for us. My aunts are real foodies and know everything there is to know about wine. They served a Sancerre from France with glazed sea bass and skinny string beans, and after dinner, we smoked a joint and each told about our first girl-girl crush. Francesca was totally relaxed and adorable sharing how at eleven she gave her best friend her track trophies in exchange for a tongue kiss. We all laughed hysterically. This was my idea of good clean family fun.

Afterward, Francesca and I went back to my apartment and made-out like we'd just been released from solitary confinement. Her passion pierced my heart, rattled my sex organs. Instinctively, I buried my face in her mass of thick dark hair. She smelled like Coppertone, a salty sea breeze, and sun-baked sand all mixed together. "Being with you makes me a better person," was just one of her poignant remarks that night. Showstoppers roll off her tongue like ticker tape. But her signature trait, I have to say, is her generosity.

The steel-toed boots I'm wearing now, she found at the flea market, and since we confirmed our love over three months ago, she's bought me an electric can opener, five Fiesta plates, a rare Billie Holiday record, not to mention a trillion retro cards from the fifties, Bogie, Marilyn, Greta Garbo, that kind of cool, black-and-white shit; Francesca's a vintage snob. Francesca's one of a kind.

Whenever we went thrifting, she would follow my eyes until they landed.

One day last month when she caught me admiring a flaming-red embroidered jean jacket, she flashed me her neon grin. "Want it, baby?" I said, "Nah," because I knew she'd buy it even though she's always broke. I wanted to get it through her thick cabeza that love was enough for me.

On Valentine's Day, she handed me the silver lighter she inherited from her best bud, Ace, who overdosed at twenty-four. She gave it to me even though she hates that I smoke, and this time, I accepted. I sensed it would help her feel less tortured about Ace's death. We'd become so close I felt like I could read her mind.

Presently, Francesca is an unemployed mechanic waiting for the right garage to come along. Boy, is that girl buff! And she keeps in shape, with or without a job. "Muscle maniac," I teased her the night she got back from a marathon bike ride to Los Angeles. Without a word, she pinned me down on my living room floor and did a hundred push ups above me. For real, she could flatten a guy in seconds; I swear she could pick up a Harley engine with her bare hands.

It was extra chilly the night she returned from L.A., and we buried ourselves under several comforters, naked and in love. Being separated for a week made us feel like we were on our honeymoon. I admit I'd had a few flashes of doubt while she was away, about whether she really cared or I really cared, all that psychotic neurotic shit, which was dispelled the instant we reunited. We latched onto each other and didn't let go all night long. I was startled by the gentle way she circled my nipples with her fingertips, then used my torso as a runway. Such style, such concentration. Oh my god, no guy has ever gone down on me like that.

After sex, while staring at her wholesome green eyes that hardly ever blink, I whispered in her ear, "Come on tour with us." I'm the lead singer for 911, a rising band in San Francisco and the invitation made me feel like a rock star, like I was driving a Ferrari instead of my mom's discarded Mercury Sable. Francesca squeezed me so tight I could have died from being over-loved. "Sure," she said. "I'll be the band's chauffeur. I'll be anything you want me to be."

The next morning, I couldn't resist calling Aunt Nikki to tell her how in love I was. She said, "Deb and I really enjoyed Francesca–a beautiful girl, with a bit of a wild streak. Am I right?"

Of course, Aunt Nikki was right. Francesca is a saint when she's sober, but all my friends at the club warned me that she was a hotheaded Chilean.

"Amanda, watch out for her jealous rages after half a dozen tequila shooters," they said. "The girl packs a violent streak."

I told them, "Chill. You don't know anything about girl love." How could I explain what a tender heart lurked beneath her South American machisma? The way she made me feel was untranslatable. Besides, I'm the last chick you need to worry about when it comes to abuse issues. I don't take shit. I learned that lesson eons ago watching my mom be mowed down by a series of losers who took advantage because she couldn't bear to be alone. Not my chosen methodology. Ultimately, I fly solo. Don't crowd me could be my slogan or bumper sticker or whatever. Freedom is my middle name. Lift a finger and I walk.

Last year, before Francesca, I loved Justin, not for real, because it was just a series of one-night stands between a singer and her tenor sax. We were both unattached restless musicians, playing in a series of dives, no cover, bullshit tips. We consoled each other by fucking after hours. No biggie. Now he's practically living with my best friend Piper, who'd die if she found out we've fucked lately, three times, all purely by accident. If we'd planned it, we'd have used a condom, so don't start. It's part of the music biz. Everything happens before you have time to reevaluate.

Francesca went snowshoeing with her brother at Tahoe for a week. 911 was in severe rehearsals, getting ready for our big breakthrough performance: opening at the legendary Fillmore in April. Naturally, we were all thinking, what if they don't like us? What if we suck? These are typical, fucked up thoughts that swirl through an artist's pre-performance mind. Personally I need my wine, my smokes, and my music buds super close by.

Anyway, our first betrayal was completely spontaneous in the sunken tub at our manager's ultra condo on "Snob" Hill. Drop dead views of Alcatraz. Justin and I were loaded on Australian Shiraz and Mendocino Sativa, so we did it skin to skin, like the total asses that we are. I've always thought Justin was gorgeous with his angelic, near-death look, septum ring, and crimson, slicked-back hair. No one can resist him. Just ask around.

The second time I can't remember, and the third was actually under the freeway in an unexpected downpour at 3 a.m., if you can believe the stupidity. Cops probably circulating like ants a few feet away. Sloppy drunk after belting cosmos at The Back Alley, we made-out like love slaves in a noir flick, laughed till we choked, and stumbled out of his Sierra pickup. Check it out: me sprawled across his dented silver fender with my kinderwhore lacy red dress up around my shoulders, him drilling away like he might strike oil, his old torn Levis sliding down his skinny pale ass, cowboy boots sunk into the mud. I thought I heard gunshots, but Justin whispered, "Don't worry, babe, it's just some biker dude backfiring," and he held me close against his rock-hard chest, while stroking my ratty hair. After that I felt more alert and scared, almost watched, but also protected by Justin's hot, calloused hands.

It was insane what we were doing. Trust me, I'm not totally unconscious. I was freezing my tits off, listening to cars whiz by overhead, rain splattering on the hood, shellacking the finish as we grunted, groaned, and sank deeper into the mud until, in true bucking bronco fashion, Justin tumbled off of me. A wet, wild rodeo! Sometimes things get started and you just can't stop them. Like dominoes. Like a million things. I'm sure there's a sophisticated physics law that explains how things go out of control, how they fall apart. But I suck at physics. And I suck at love. Does it count that the whole time with Justin I was missing Francesca?

I'd never be Justin's girlfriend. Number one because he's with Piper now, but also because he cheats, moving from one random hole to the next like he's playing miniature golf. I tried to warn Piper when she first got crushed out on him. We were at O'Toole's last Christmas Eve, shooting pool, and Justin had gone to the bar for beers. I whispered, "Pipe, you're in psychotic denial if you think he'll be faithful for five minutes." She set her eyes on me with an optometrist's concentration. "Amanda, we love each other." Please! I thought, but I hugged her.

Despite her ignorance, I love Piper like a sister, and I'll be there for her when Justin dumps her, which statistically should be in six months max, even though he'll never do any better than her. What a looker, what poise. Fucking rad with hot pink Betty Page bangs. Piper is a nasty girl with balls. Girls with balls are the exact opposite of boys with balls. With girls, it's like a diabetic taking insulin; with boys it's equivalent to giving a bull testosterone shots. When I'm hungover or tied up in rehearsal, she's the first one in line to fill in for me at the restaurant. My boss loves her. Everyone at work does. For example, I can call her at 6 a.m. and she'll show up at Mel's Drive-In at 7 with her smile intact, even if she's bartended at The Red Room the night before. Awesome chick. A rare breed. I can tell Piper stuff I can't tell anyone else, and she listens without attitude. Like when I blurted the news about Francesca and me. "Good for you," she said, scrunching up her lovely face in happiness. That's true friendship. "Anyone gives you trouble, send them to me." She winked adorably. That was back when we were both newly love-struck and monogamous. She squeezed me tight and we cried. I thought, Piper is the best friend a girl could ever have.

Of course I feel guilty about Justin! What kind of rotten person betrays a genuine friend, and her amazing new girl lover? First of all, even though I realize it's not a real defense, I always think of Justin as Piper's boyfriend, not mine. Plus, each time we do it, I swear to God it's the last time. I guess I'm addicted to lust, or just scared shitless of emptiness. Maybe I'm like those people who buy more insurance then they'll ever need just so they can sleep at night. As far as cheating on Francesca, I have no fucking excuse. So mostly, I don't let myself think about it. It's how a coward copes. It would tear me apart if I admitted how goddamn weak and selfish I am. Tough on the outside with a camouflaged soul. If I let that mushy center ooze out, I just might have to take Thorazine and go to bed for a thousand years.

Wine helps. Dope definitely helps. And making music temporarily erases all fears without nasty side effects. Most recently, loving a girl had felt like taking a Valium laced with ecstasy. It was a new thing for me, and I got totally into it. I felt pried wide open. My insatiable curiosity about girl love turned out to reveal the very best part of me. Until the big fight.

Saturday night. Fucking mega-opening night at the Fillmore. Everyone in the band was a nervous wreck. Francesca came along for support and kept bringing us shots backstage while we warmed up. I could tell she didn't like it that I needed hugs from Justin, and that he periodically rubbed my shoulders and kissed the top of my head. It's just what we do before we go on. It's how our band gets by. It's the biz. Francesca just didn't comprehend the stress a musician is under psyching up for a gig. Thank god, the crowd loved us. We were high as skyscrapers. Justin picked me up and twirled me around about a hundred times. Even our semi-autistic drummer hugged me.

When Francesca and I got back to my apartment, she started spewing accusations about the sleazy way I leaned on Justin between sets. She was so loaded she said crazy shit like that I love the band, especially Justin, way more than her.

"You're doing him, aren't you, bitch?" she screamed, standing two inches from my face. Staring at her plump lips and wild Latin hair, I tried to talk her down, but it was as if I was speaking Swahili.

"Why are you fucking with my head?" she cried. I clamped my hands onto the sides of her curly dark head to keep it from shaking from side to side, and said, "Francesca, you're fucking drunk. Trust me, I love you. But you're bringing me down!" You can't say I didn't try.

"Then why were you making out with Justin backstage?" she hollered. She crossed her arms and squinted like a snake in the sun.

"What are you talking about?" I yelled, but she slammed my face against the door, and I thought, oh shit, this is going to leave one super-sized black eye!

"Damn, now you've gone and done it, fucking crazy Francesca." She'd hit me; how could I be with her? What about my values? My self-respect? I had my reputation to uphold. I know–what kind of fucking reputation do I have to protect? Well, everyone has their bottom line. When all the people who mattered in my world saw my banged up face, they'd start broadcasting negative reviews. I would be their tragic heroine. I would reek of victimization. I could already hear their chorus of "I told you so, Amanda," and "Girl, whatever happened to your non-violence policy?"

Francesca stood there crying like an orphan; snot came out of her nose and her mouth. I could see she was scared to death I wouldn't forgive her, and that she hated herself for the violent act she'd just committed. Still I couldn't resist rattling off every mean and self-righteous thing I could think of about her messing with my freedom, and my face. What did she expect, fucking sympathy, just because she was bawling? I threw an Academy Award-winning tantrum.

"Get the hell out of here," I said as a finale, and locked myself in the bathroom. When I came out she was gone. The silence was deafening. I put ice on my face, chugged burgundy out of the bottle, then inhaled half a joint in one drag.

Good for you, girl. I gave myself a gold medal for having healthy boundaries, as my mom now calls "drawing the line," after three years in recovery. Maybe I should go to an Al-Anon meeting with her, I thought; then decided, no, too drastic–after all, I'm only twenty-three. Instead, I marched around the empty apartment like a coked-up hit man, screaming, "It's over, you fucking bitch Francesca!" I coughed, started crying, hiccupping, and heaving until

I collapsed on the bed in a slobbering heap of self-pity. Typical fucking April. The cruelest month!

After a while, I felt cleansed in a reborn kind of way. I picked up my guitar, planning to write a brilliant bluesy rock tune about how love is more brutal than a car crash, when Justin strolled in like he always does when Piper's working nights at The Red Room. This twenty-four-hour open-door policy is Justin's idea of band privilege. "What shit happened to you, girl?" He retracted his chin. "Forget about it," I said, and passed him the joint. He raised his hands in surrender.

It's late now, it's the middle of the fucking night and we're on our second AMC movie. Bette Davis is reading the riot act to some clean-cut dude who can't get a word in edgewise. Both of them smoking as though they'd just as soon have sex with their cigarettes as each other.

I'm floating somewhere between drunk and hung-over. My left cheek and eye are hot, pulsing, with a nasty bruise rising. Justin's slung across my bed like a six-foot long mop. Leaning on one elbow, I stare at Bette doing outraged, while the cool cucumber in the pale grey suit is blowing clouds of smoke in her face.

"She's on fire," Justin says, after playing dead for half an hour. Not even a twitch comes from that boy's torso.

Without taking his eyes off the screen, he begins to massage my neck and back. His fingers dance across my skin like it's a keyboard and he's a secretary dreaming of becoming a ballet dancer. Finally, he shifts down along my thigh, casually, slipping his finger in with the grace of a tomcat doing yoga.

I've got my mouth on Justin, but I could gag. Thinking about Francesca's 100 per cent authentic smile, I can barely concentrate on his stiff cock. This shit has got to stop. Tears are spilling all over his balls, but he's holding my head down.

All I can think about is the first night Francesca and I made love and she looked at me with those clear green eyes and said, "I haven't opened up this much to anyone in four years." She was shaking and pale when she said it, and still, holding onto me tight. Nobody, not Justin, not Piper, not even my mom, who I adore, has ever revealed their true self to me like that. Her gorgeous Latin face got all blurry and chubby with vulnerability; that's the pure South American girl I fell in love with and couldn't get out of my head. When we were alone, the rest of my life evaporated.

By the time I'm spitting Justin out–I just can't swallow that shit tonight–I'm tripping on Francesca big time. Her hands gently skiing over my breasts, her melting eyes never leaving mine when we come together in rapturous waves of girl lust. Reliving those moments gives me the chills, like I just caught the flu from thinking too much about lost love.

Lying there, essentially alone, I'm reflecting on recent history. I mean, really! Going at it again with Justin, after Francesca and I shared the most erotic encounters of our lives? Blending together like one person instead of just the usual rocking and rolling. And look at Justin now. He's a corpse compared with Francesca. Not even a hug after sex.

It's not hard to get his lazy ass out of here; it's time for him to go pick up Piper at The Red Room, so he can bang the hell out of her before he passes out again. Good luck, girlfriend! I feel sorry for Piper.

As soon as Justin's out the door, I consider going over to Aunt Nikki's for comfort. She'll see the black eye, and without a word will hand me an ice pack. But why should I lay this shit on her? I need to clean up my own messes. It's time to grow up for real, girl.

I check my cell phone messages. "Hi, it's me baby. Please don't hang up." Francesca sounds 1000 percent sincere and endearing; I choke up and melt a little deeper down. "I can't believe I hit you," she goes on. "I guess I'm too in love. I got crazy thinking of you doing it with somebody else, but you're right, it's your body, your freedom and I respect that totally. I'm going to cure myself of jealousy. I swear. I'll go to therapy five days a week, stop drinking, maybe even volunteer at my church. Whatever you want. I won't let you down."

By then tears are bouncing off my naked tits and I'm punching call return. "Hey, Francesca, it's me," I tell her when she picks up. I feel seismic love waves radiate from the epicenter of my heart. "I fucked up too," I tell her. "It was wrong what I did. Maybe it's me who owes you an apology."

"No way," she says, hiccupping.

"Way," I answer back, discarding my pride like the useless appendage it is. It's a hell of a lot easier to forgive a hot temper than a full-time frozen heart.

Recovery

They were eating their oatmeal and drinking their morning coffee when Kim threw a potholder at the kitchen wall. "We're squandering our youth!!" she blurted as the potholder dropped limply to the floor.

"Squandering? What are you talking about?" Frannie asked, startled out of checking her stock portfolio online.

"We're like our parents. We don't talk at breakfast. We don't have sex and we don't have fun."

"What about Denise's party? That was fun. And we had sex when we got home. I remember, it was hot," Frannie said, building her case. Denise was Kim's boss at the art gallery.

"That was three months ago."

"Three months isn't that long, when you consider how busy we've been."

"You're the workaholic, not me," Kim muttered.

Where was all this combative shit coming from? They were forty-one. Not kids. They had responsibilities, commitments. A mortgage for Christ's sake! Today Frannie had seven therapy patients and an hour commute across the Golden Gate Bridge. Wasn't that enough stress for one person to cope with? Kim's moodiness was out of character, given her dedicated yoga and meditation practice.

"Things naturally slow down after seven years," was the best Frannie could come up with to stave off domestic war. She needed to get the hell out of there. "Fallow periods are normal in any relationship."

"Fallow? What bullshit," Kim crossed her arms and sulked.

"Okay. Let's start over. What are we doing tonight?"

"Nothing. As usual."

"How about we cook together and fool around? We'll have fun." Frannie winked, and seeing Kim's smile bloom, she knew she'd finessed a truce. "Gotta run, babe. My nine o'clock is a real piece of work." As she headed out the door, clutching her car keys, she felt the anticipation of the evening ahead grow knotty vines into her heart. "Looking forward to tonight!" she shouted.

Nine hours later with no real break between clients, and only a power bar for lunch, Frannie pulled into the driveway of their Mill Valley bungalow and watched Kim's shadow glide behind the kitchen shutters.

"Pasta, okay?" Kim looked up from mincing garlic as Frannie strolled in with a bottle of wine. Wasn't it a little late to ask about the pasta?

"Vino," Frannie said, handing over the old vine Zinfindel.

"You splurged," Kim said, staring at the frolicking forest nymphs on the wine label. Her shiny auburn hair was out of its clip, framing her kiwi green eyes, flushed cheeks and bright smile. All that pranayama made her seem perpetually horny. Frannie barely had time for a run these days, and the only time she thought about sex was when she was on the massage table.

Kim had laid out a platter of olives, artichoke hearts, burrata and a baguette on the dining room table. Red roses from their garden brushed up against two slender white tapers ready to be torched. Well, didn't she think of everything! Suddenly, the old vine Zin didn't seem noteworthy. So what? Frannie's passions lay not in mastering recipes or creating the perfect feng shui décor, but in unearthing people's internal process, dealing with all the deep messy stuff.

She caught a glimpse of herself in the hall mirror, and was struck by her unkempt hair and pale complexion. She'd have to take a shower before they got into bed, if that was where this night was leading. Three months since they'd had sex? They used to joke about lesbian bed-death, never imagining it happening to them!

Frannie opened the wine and poured a glass for each of them. "Looks like you've done everything," she said.

"You can just relax," Kim smiled, peeling an onion.

"I am relaxed," Frannie snapped. "It's just that I thought we were going to cook together. Wasn't that the plan?" Kim's eyes filled with tears. Had she ruined things already? "What's wrong?"

"It's just the onions," Kim said unconvincingly.

Frannie decided to ignore the crying and start the salad. While gathering an armful of greens from the fridge, her cell phone vibrated in her pocket. Could be Emily, her recovering coke addict who'd blown off her appointment today. Waiting in her office at four p.m, Frannie had listened to the minutes click by on the wall clock like strained heartbeats. She wondered if she'd missed something about this girl who'd only been sober for two months. Maybe she'd pushed too hard when she suggested daily NA meetings. If Emily killed herself would it be her fault? Frannie's mind stuck like Velcro to the possibility of professional failure. She desperately needed to do the right thing, and not lose anyone.

The phone call was from Judy, a less worrisome patient, inquiring about the time of her next session. When they hung up, Frannie shrugged in Kim's direction, acknowledging her phone crime. "I only picked up because of Emily. You know, I'm worried she might start using again."

"Actually, no. I didn't know." Kim reached for her wine glass and gave Frannie a look that registered as a warning. Frannie felt scrutinized, judged. It was too much pressure this whole thing about fun and sex, especially on a Friday night. It wasn't natural to drop every single concern in life just because it was the fucking weekend.

As Kim cleaned mushrooms, Frannie poured a second glass of wine. "I just want to know if she's alive. So we can kick back."

"I can kick back without knowing," Kim said. Turning toward the cutting board, she began to chop off the heads of shitakes.

Frannie sliced open an avocado and plucked out its pit. The rim was blackened, so she scraped off the dark edges and rescued the rest. The silence only exaggerated her loneliness. Maybe everything was hopeless after all.

"I can't just stand by and let Emily kill herself!" she blurted.

"How are you going to stop her?" Kim asked, dropping handfuls of rigatoni into the boiling water.

If Frannie couldn't salvage the evening, what kind of partner was she? She couldn't bear to be one of those therapists who help couples reconcile but end up miserable and alone themselves.

"Kim, I got home as soon as I could. I brought your favorite Zin. I love you. What do you want me to do?"

"Come over here," Kim said, softening, and Frannie was happy to fall into her arms.

After dinner, Frannie took a shower and tried to hold onto the warm cozy feeling from the wine. But drying off, she had the sudden urge to get in her car and drive away, go someplace where she couldn't disappoint anyone. She reminded herself that Kim wasn't her critical, demanding mother. Nothing like her. She was safe with Kim. Kim loved her wholeheartedly and gave her all the freedom she required.

She pulled on a white undershirt, brushed her teeth until her gums bled, and took a deep belly breath. Then she joined Kim in the bedroom who was bent over, lighting candles on the window ledge. Her long muscular back and round butt produced a compelling landscape. Frannie was aware of something pleasant stirring inside her. When Kim downloaded Amy Winehouse, they lay down on the bed beside each other, and listened to the soulful sounds alter the energy in the room. Frannie tracked Kim's breath, trying to adopt its steady rhythm. Relieved to be horizontal, she turned to Kim, admiring her full lips and delicate earlobes with all those shiny hoops.

"Sorry I was hyper when I came home," Frannie offered, as her limbs gravitated towards Kim's like a plant to light. "Sometimes transitioning is rough."

"You give too much," Kim said, as she reached over to the nightstand drawer and removed a plastic bag, then rolled a joint, lit it, took a drag, and passed it to Frannie. Frannie chose to let the comment go by.

Maybe getting stoned would kick-start her libido. She took a deep drag. Sure enough the combo of the music and dope began to blur the tension and even the ghost of Emily dissolved into a puffball of smoke. Nerves of pleasure running along Frannie's spine woke up the way they had seven years before when their bodies rocked with lust. Without any prompting, she reached over and kissed Kim full on, and unexpectedly, gratefully, time and space split open and devoured them.

When her cell phone rang at 9:27, Frannie raised her hands in the air as if held at gunpoint. "See? I'm not picking up!"

"Congratulations!" Kim laughed.

Frannie leaned on one elbow. "Kim, do you really think I'm a workaholic? Should I give up evenings or maybe only work four-day weeks?"

Kim held Frannie's shoulders down. "Shut up, Frances. Or I'll have to handcuff you!"

Only because she was stoned could she relinquish her line of questioning. Fuck work, she thought. Fuck Emily. Fuck everything except this. Then they began to touch each other in long-neglected places. Frannie was electrified. How could she have let all this pleasure go?

Her cell rang again at 10:09. "It's late. I better get it," Frannie said.

"Probably Emily," Kim muttered.

As she listened to the caller, Frannie grew pale and held her breath. Sensing trouble, Kim wrapped her arms around Frannie. "Who is it baby? What's wrong?"

"My mother," Frannie answered, trembling. "She fell and broke something. They took her by ambulance to St. John's in Santa Monica. I've got to get down there." And then she started to pack.

Before she flew to LA, Frannie notified her patients, and promised Kim she would check in every night. She still hadn't heard from Emily, but that concern was relegated to the back burner.

At St John's Hospital, Frannie followed a maze of hallways to her mother's room in the recovery unit. Not knowing what to expect, she was relieved to find Estelle sleeping peacefully. As usual, Frannie had imagined the worst. Wearing the standard blue gown, stripped of makeup and jewelry, Estelle at seventy-nine seemed a little older, but intact and not in discernible pain.

A pretty, voluptuous black nurse came in and informed Frannie that the surgery had gone so well that they'd transferred her mother directly to Rehab.

"She's adorable," the nurse told Frannie. "Sweet as sugar."

Frannie smiled and thought, Wait. Wait until she wakes up.

Hours later, after Frannie had taken a walk at the beach and grabbed a sandwich in the cafeteria, she returned to her mother's room to find Estelle propped up on pillows looking miraculously alert.

"Finally you made it!" Estelle said. Whatever pain medication she was on hadn't dulled the intensity of her gaze.

"I've been here for hours, Mom. You were asleep."

"I've never seen so many black nurses at St. John's," Estelle announced, "but they've been nice to me." Frannie felt a familiar electrical charge at the back of her head.

"Yes. Everyone seems nice. I'm so sorry about your fall, Mom. What a bummer."

"I'm an old woman, Frances. It's normal for these things to happen. Oh look!" Estelle's attention was drawn to the hallway. "That fat, colored nurse must weigh three hundred pounds. In her profession you'd think she'd take better care of herself. I guess these people don't worry about their health the way we do. Maybe they're better off!"

"Mom!" Another jolt, this time to the solar plexus. "That nurse just told me how much she likes you."

"She can't hear me, Frances. Anyway, what did I say that was so wrong?"

"Nothing." It was impossible to argue with her mother, the woman who had shaped her feelings of inadequacy, confusion and rage. She poured hot water over a Lipton's teabag in a tiny Styrofoam cup and handed it to Estelle. Then, she straightened the sheets around her mother's shoulders, organized the medicine bottles on the side table, and with nothing left to fix, sat down on a hard plastic chair. She wanted a drink, a stiff one.

"I'm glad you're here," Estelle said in her typically disarming change of tone. "I told your sister not to come. She's got enough problems with that rotten husband of hers."

"Rachel's not coming?" Frannie had naturally assumed her sister would be there within hours. She always came when there was a family emergency. Always! She was the good one in a crisis. Born with a coated nervous system that coped easily with Estelle's erratic moods and unreasonable demands. The buffer for Frannie's discomfort.

"She can't leave Jennifer in New York with Howard, not with the way things are." Estelle sighed.

"What things?" Frannie said, trying to control the rising panic in her voice.

"Rachel suspects Howard is shtupping his secretary."

"She's not coming at all?"

"I'm too much trouble for you girls. Maybe it's time I joined Daddy," she said, glancing up at the acoustic ceiling as if communing with her dead husband, Morris. "Then you could live in peace," Estelle said. Within seconds, she folded her arms across her chest and fell asleep.

That night at her mother's house, Frannie drank half a bottle of a Malbec along with a take-out cheeseburger and fries. Exhausted and a little drunk, she forgot about her promise to call Kim. By the time she remembered, it was 11:30–too late. She curled up in her childhood twin bed, and watched an old movie until she fell into a deep sleep.

The following morning, after a long run on the beach, Frannie arrived at Estelle's room, pumped.

"I didn't sleep," Estelle said. "That Oriental woman's family planted themselves on the floor until midnight." She was referring to the octogenarian with a fractured shoulder who now occupied the adjacent bed in the room. "They ate out of cartons and talked Chinese so nobody could understand them. Now the room stinks of fried rice. Smell it?"

Frannie opened the curtains to let in the sunlight, determined to create an uplifting atmosphere. "You look good, Mom. Your color is back."

"You think so? Hand me the mirror," Estelle said, and passed the remote to Frannie. "Put on 'The View.'" Estelle watched Whoopi Goldberg welcome Angelina

Jolie onto the show. They were discussing the rewards of adopting orphans from third-world countries, lifting them out of unbearable circumstances.

"They might be carrying some foreign disease," Estelle said directly to the TV screen. "Personally, I wouldn't take a chance."

"Not even if you could make a difference in their lives?" Frannie asked.

"You still could catch something terrible," her mother said.

Beginning on Monday, Frannie met with Estelle's social worker, stayed in close touch with the doctors and nurses, made sure everyone did their job while trying to keep her mother from offending anyone. She monitored the medication, brought in deli sandwiches, and kept her mother company watching "Seinfeld" reruns. At home, she watered straggly plants, paid bills, and fetched her mother's various relics: cold cream, bobby pins, Metamucil and mustache bleach. She was on task and bone tired by the end of each day. She kept her phone calls with Kim short and practical.

Rachel phoned her to say that Howard had agreed to couple's counseling.

"Fantastic," Frannie said in a stupor of Dos Equis and stale tortilla chips. She wondered if she and Kim should be in therapy.

"I appreciate you taking over, Frannie. I'll make it up to you."

"Just give Howard hell, and I'll consider myself compensated."

On day number four, Estelle complained her hair was dirty and her nails were chipped. Frannie set up appointments with a visiting hairdresser and a manicurist. "Go home and relax while I have my treatments," Estelle instructed her. "You did everything already. You're just like your father. Rachel's a sweet girl but she walks in circles." Nobody got off the hook.

Back at the house, Frannie sunk into a cushy chaise lounge in the backyard, and soaked up the afternoon sun. She recalled her last night with Kim. How close they'd gotten, how promising everything had seemed. Suddenly, she didn't want to wait until evening to speak again. She decided to phone the gallery immediately and tell Kim she missed her because suddenly she did!

"How's your mother?" Kim asked in a distracted tone.

"Is this a bad time?" Frannie asked.

"Denise and I are hanging paintings for the show, but no, tell me how you are?"

Five years ago, when Denise hired Kim, Denise was living with Sherry and the two couples had become good friends, but Denise was single now and looking.

"Are you okay with me being in LA?" Frannie asked. "You sound a little weird."

"No, I'm just hungover," Kim said. "Denise and I went out with the artist last night and I had one too many cosmos." Frannie heard Denise in the background, and then muffled laughter.

"Denise says 'Hi.'" More laughter. "By the way, honey, she invited us up to her cabin this weekend. Wanna go?"

"Afraid I won't be back. Mom needs me here a couple of extra days since Rachel isn't coming."

"Okay with you if I go?"

"I'd be a bitch if I said no. Tell Denise thanks for the invite. Another time, yeah?" When she hung up, Frannie felt empty. She'd forgotten to tell Kim how much she missed her.

Estelle improved daily, did her physical therapy like a trooper. "How's Kim?" she asked one day during a commercial between soap operas. "Is she still painting those interesting pictures?"

Estelle rarely brought up Kim, though they had always gotten along well enough. Estelle simply didn't show much interest in any of the people in Frannie's world. She was preoccupied with her own concerns. So Frannie took this as an opening even though her mother's use of the word "interesting" was undeniably ambiguous.

"Working at the gallery, there's not much time to paint, Mom." What else could she say? That they were having a rough patch? That she didn't have a clue about how to be a satisfying partner? She couldn't trust her mother with that much personal information.

"You girls work too much," Estelle said. "In my day, only the men drove themselves crazy with work."

"Well, frankly Mom, we don't have that luxury, seeing as there is no man in our household."

Estelle changed the subject, nodding toward Mrs. Jang, who was snoring loudly. "She's nutty. All night she talks to ghosts. Then at the crack of dawn, the family arrives with their commotion. The slim night nurse told me one of her sons is a big shot Hollywood director. What's his name, he's famous...? Anyway, he's too busy to visit his eighty-nine-year-old mother."

"Shame on him!" Frannie said.

Estelle shifted her gaze toward the wall clock. "They're having a special dinner tonight with entertainment. 'Cabaret Night,' they call it. Come. It'll be fun." Fun. The magic word.

Frannie ducked into the courtyard to phone Kim's cell but there was no answer, so she left a message. "Hi, baby. Just thinking about you."

Right after she hung up, Rachel called.

"Turns out it's his yoga teacher," Rachel shouted. "He's been lying to me for a year, and I encouraged him to take those fucking yoga classes, to unwind!"

"You don't deserve this, Rachel."

"I know." Rachel sniffled. "He's begging me to forgive him. If it wasn't for Jennifer, I'd probably divorce him." Frannie doubted that. She also couldn't imagine Howard begging for anything, or anyone forgiving a year of infidelity and lies.

"Oh Frannie, you must be so sick of hearing about my problems. Tell me, how are you and Kim doing?" Rachel asked.

"According to Kim we haven't had fun in months."

"I thought lesbians got along better than heteros."

"Well, they don't."

When Frannie returned to Estelle's room, her mother had applied foundation, powder and lipstick. "See," she said, showing off her glossy red smile. "I'm not completely helpless."

Frannie helped Estelle into her silk kimono, then lowered her into the wheelchair and pushed her down the hallway to Cabaret Night.

"You're wearing jeans to a party?" Estelle asked.

"I wasn't going to go home to change clothes for ninety-year-olds in bathrobes." Frannie's anxiety was turning to meanness.

When they arrived in the overheated dining room, which smelled like meat loaf and disinfectant, she parked her mother beside an Alan Alda look-alike in a blue running suit. Frannie stood behind her mother's wheelchair, waiting for an opportunity to escape into the fresh air.

"He's a gym user, like Daddy." Estelle whispered.

"Welcome to the world of aches and pains and potato chip hors d'oeuvres, ladies," the handsome stranger bellowed and extended his hand. "I'm Jerome."

Her mother blushed. "Estelle Stein. This is my brainy daughter, Frances. She's a psychologist. Be careful she doesn't try to figure you out. What's wrong with you?" Estelle asked Jerome. "You look so fit."

"Fell out of an airplane," Jerome answered, and they both laughed.

"I need to call a client," Frannie announced. "Have fun." As she left, she heard Jerome ask, "Where is she going?"

"That kid," Estelle answered. "She can't sit still."

Outside in the garden, the citrus smells and balmy night air sharpened Frannie's longing for Kim. She checked her cell phone. The only message was from Emily saying she was sorry about missing her session. She sounded sober, even happy. All that worry for nothing.

Frannie thought about phoning Kim, but she and Denise were probably still on the road. Besides, she didn't want to appear desperate. She'd wait until after they'd arrived at the cabin and settled in. Looking up at the sliver of moonlight, Frannie experienced a twinge of fear. She hoped they'd be careful driving up that twisty mountain road in the dark.

Standing in the doorway, Frannie saw that Jerome and Estelle's snowy white heads had drifted together like cumulous clouds. They were crooning "The White Cliffs of Dover," along with the pianist and half a dozen other patients. They were like children who randomly collide on the playground and become each other's best friend. Was everyone capable of fun but her?

Soaking in the bathtub that night, Frannie analyzed Kim's motives for going with Denise to her decrepit Tahoe cabin for a retreat. She and Kim had gone there only once when Kim was still with Sally, and they had joked about how funky it was. "Why does Denise always invite us when I have other plans?" Frannie had asked. "Pure coincidence," Kim answered. "No, Kim. It's because she has a crush on you!" "Well, I've never gone without you, have I?" Kim replied.

She called again. No answer. Maybe they'd stopped for dinner at a restaurant where there was no reception. Take a breath, she told herself. Calm the fuck down. Frannie couldn't remember exactly how long the trip up to the cabin was, but she imagined it was a slow trek, especially with the weekend crunch. And why should they rush? They were on vacation. But what about Denise's drinking? Hopefully she hadn't downed a couple of strong Bloodys, then crashed into a tree. This was crazy thinking. She just missed Kim, that was all. Maybe after an arduous drive, they'd gone straight to sleep. Then Frannie obsessed about the sleeping arrangements. How many bedrooms, how many beds? She couldn't remember. Her mind was tilted at a dangerous angle.

Frannie decided to call once more and leave a message. "Guess where I am right now?" She tried to sound casual. "In the tub! Are you proud of me? She splashed some water loudly and added, "Hear that! I'm relaxing. Call me, okay? I miss you!"

She would call again first thing in the morning, before Kim got up or went anywhere. She would tell her how much she loved her and that she was going to be a better partner when she returned home.

But the next morning at seven a.m. sharp, there still was no answer. On the way to the hospital, Frannie stopped at Starbucks. Standing in line, she pressed redial. "Hi! It's me. I'm starting to worry." Where in the hell could she be this early? In the shower? Out hiking already? Wherever she was, Denise was with her.

"Where have you been? I was starting to worry." Estelle sat in a chair in her room, picking at a fruit cup. Frannie stared at her mother's lavish bouffant hairdo and long painted fingernails, bright red to match her lips. She was certain no one had ever looked so put together, so glamorous in a rehab facility.

"Traffic," Frannie lied.

"I've got enough to worry about with Rachel. Why she married him I'll never know."

"Maybe it was the eleven million," Frannie suggested.

"Rachel isn't materialistic. In her own way, she loves him. She doesn't deserve such rotten treatment."

"No one does, Mother."

"What's with you today?" Estelle asked, pushing her breakfast away.

"Nothing. Howard's just such an asshole."

"We never liked him either," Estelle declared, meaning she and Morris, who had died of cancer two years before. It was a rare moment of intimacy between mother and daughter.

"Don't get me wrong. I'm glad they're in therapy. Maybe they'll finally deal with their crap one way or the other."

"You and your therapy! People don't change, Francis. I don't understand your generation. Always analyzing everything, instead of just living. You were such a happy kid."

"I'm happy now," Frannie shouted, sounding miserable even to herself.

"Don't try to save the world. It will only wear you out," Estelle said.

Back at her mother's house, she curled up on her bed, and pulled the comforter up around her shoulders. She lay still, staring at her cell phone, willing it to ring. In the excruciating quiet, she couldn't avoid the dread that arose in her. Her mounting jealousy and suspicion about Kim and Denise reminded her of her most needy, paranoid patients who ultimately drove their lovers away. Maybe Kim was planning to leave her. Maybe Frannie had neglected her one too many times. She called again. This time the voicemail was full. A good thing, since she was so strung out she'd probably say things she'd regret.

Just then her cell phone rang. A miracle. An answered prayer. Frannie sprinted, almost tripped over the ottoman in the den.

"We saw the therapist," Rachel said. "Howard cried. I haven't seen him cry since our wedding. And when we got home, he apologized to Jessica for being a shitty father. Not bad, for one session, right, Doc? Are you there, Frannie?"

"Yes. That's great, Rach. I'm happy for you." Frannie had to get off the phone. The only person she wanted to speak to was Kim.

"When are you leaving?"

"Mom's released on Sunday, so I'll leave right after I get her settled at home."

"You must be dying to see Kim."

"I just hope she wants to see me."

"You're nuts, Fran. Kim is crazy about you."

Frannie made plane reservations for Sunday evening. She would go home and wait for Kim to return from Tahoe. Then she would find out what had gone wrong.

On Saturday morning, Mrs. Jang was having difficulty breathing. Estelle told Frannie that her rotten director son still hadn't shown up. "A shanda." The rest of her family continued to come: sisters, brothers, even distant cousins. The relatives' children chased each other in and out of the room, playing games as if they were at a birthday party. Estelle seemed to have gotten accustomed to the clatter, the way one gets used to a train going by.

"So, you go home tomorrow, Mom. Me too."

"Marvelous. Soon I'll be sitting in my living room talking to Dr. Phil."

"Well, you could talk to Ellen instead!" Frannie joked. "I'm sure Rachel will be visiting soon, now that she's straightened things out at home."

"I hope she doesn't bring that son-of-a gun," Estelle said.

Sunday morning, Frannie arrived early at the hospital with a suitcase to pack up her mother's belongings. The caregiver was meeting them at the house at one p.m.

"She died," Estelle announced when Frannie entered the room. The empty bed was already freshly made-up with clean white sheets for the next patient. According to the on-duty nurse, Mrs. Jang had suffered cardiac arrest during the night. Estelle was visibly shaken. Clearly her vulnerability had been pierced by the closeness of death.

"I asked the colored nurse to sit with me after it happened. I was shook up. Do you know what she said? She said, 'Don't you want to wait until a skinny white nurse comes on duty?' and she walked out of the room. She just left me here. What kind of a nurse treats her patients like that? Anyway, I'm next."

"Mom! You have a broken leg. You'll be good as new."

"Her son never got to see her, " Estelle said, looking frightened.

Frannie sat on the bed beside her mother and took her hand. "I'm glad I came."

"Me too." Estelle regained her composure. "I'll be fine. Don't worry about me. By the way, Jerome took my phone number." Estelle smiled. "Maybe we'll go out to dinner or to the movies. He's nothing like Daddy. But at least he has a car."

"Well, that's essential for dating in LA."

"Do you think he likes me?" Estelle seemed suddenly shy like a schoolgirl.

"I think what really matters, Mom, is do you like him?"

Estelle squeezed Frannie's hand and looked directly into her eyes. "You're a good kid. You helped me out."

"Thanks, Mom." Frannie took a moment to consider what she was about to say. "I'm thinking of asking Kim to marry me when I get home. I think it's time."

"Good for you. Marriage is a wonderful institution."

"Would you come to the wedding?"

"I wouldn't miss it. I just wish Daddy could come. He loved weddings."

Frannie pulled up a chair close to her mother's and turned on The View. The show's guest was Jeff Bridges, who had been married to the same woman throughout his career. Both Estelle and Frannie agreed this was a wonderful accomplishment and that Bridges was a rare and exceptional man.

"Especially since people in show business always cheat," Estelle remarked.

"There's always the exception, Mom," Frannie said, praying that she would be given a second chance to show Kim the appreciation she deserved.

On her way to the airport, Frannie received a text from Kim. "Hi babe. Lost my phone. Using Denise's. Didn't want you to worry. Be back Sunday night, probably between 8 and 9. See you then." And she had added a single red heart emoji. That was it. Indecipherable. Insane. Even her clients would have left a more personal message.

Frannie's mind went wild trying to interpret the text. Was it a pre-breakup message? Or was Kim simply being neutral because it was Denise's phone? Or had they written the note together, strategizing about how to let Frannie down easy? Or maybe, it was just another of those times when she imagined the worst-case scenario and everything was really all right between them. She'd have to wait to see Kim in person to discover her fate. Frannie recalled Kim's remarks of the previous week. It wasn't her youth she'd been squandering. It was her whole life, her one beautiful life.

The New Restaurant

Have you been to the new restaurant?

Which restaurant?

You know the one with the hunter green awning and the French name. Everyone's talking about how amazing it is.

Haven't heard a thing.

Not only phenomenal food, but killer cocktails. You can't even get in, it's so popular.

Have you been?

Haven't been able to get a reservation.

Well, let's try tonight. Tuesday shouldn't be too bad. Maybe we'll get lucky.

You think so? Apparently the chef is from the Cordon Bleu so everything is extremely authentic.

The two friends call the new French restaurant and find out from the maître d', who sounds hurried but friendly, that their first opening is at 9:45 pm.

Is that too late for you?

No, we'll take it!
The friends are both elated and go home to take a nap.

When they arrive at L'Auberge, the place is bustling as predicted. The ambience is festive and sophisticated like an Academy Awards' party. Men and women are dressed in their finest, and are casually chatting about tennis and the ups and downs of a wild stock market while eating various parts of rabbit, duck and pig. The wine list is several pages long, impressive and indecipherable. The waiters and waitresses, with the elevated posture of dancers, are dressed in penguin black and white, and hold plates proudly above their heads, dancing through the crowd like members of a ballet company.

The outdoor fire pit and garden are beautiful. The curved mahogany bar, teak floors, and the oil paintings of Parisian cafes are beautiful. The presentation of food is so beautiful that customers hesitate to disrupt the aesthetics by taking the first bite.

Would you like a cocktail, their very own beautiful ballet dancer asks?

Oh yes, by all means, the first friend replies. I hear the cocktails are extraordinary.

Oh yes, says the handsome waiter. We are quite famous for our libations.

How could that be true? our friends wonder, since they just opened a week ago.

The lemon drops are a bit watery but artfully served in elegant martini glasses with sugar rims and spiraling lemon twists. The friends sip their drinks while studying the menu, which involves confits, coulis, bouchée and many other words they don't understand.

What do you recommend? they ask the waiter who tells them sincerely that everything on the menu is superb. The chef was trained at the Cordon Bleu, he explains with his hand placed over his heart. Trust Me! You cannot make a mistake. They take their chances on the duck a l'orange and the cassoulet.

Both dishes are smaller than expected and a little salty, though tasty in a strange European way. Perhaps they didn't make the best choice. The people at the next table have ordered coq au vin and seem deliriously happy. The friends agree that next time coq au vin it is. They acknowledge that in any new restaurant there are always kinks to work out.

The waiter suggests dessert. While on their second glass of Bordeaux, they decide what's the harm in splurging. Besides they are nowhere near full after the petit diné. They order creme bruleé to split, and two espressos. The dessert and the coffees are the size of doll furniture, but tasty and not too salty.

The bill comes to two hundred and fifty dollars, which is much higher than expected, but really, it's been more than a dinner. It's been a social event, a fête. During the two-hour meal they have run into close friends who divulge that this is their new favorite restaurant. Our friends rave as well, though secretly they feel confused.

Will you come back? one asks the other when they are outside in the fresh air walking to their car.

Will you?

Well, let's see how it does.

Exactly. After they work out the kinks.

Weeks pass and L'Auberge is continually jammed. Everyone continues to rave. After six months, however, the buzz dies down and it becomes a little easier to get a reservation. The friends call and are told they can come at 7. What if we wanted to come at 7:30? That would be fine as well, says the maître d'.

When they arrive the restaurant is half full but the staff is still high-spirited.

The friends skip the puny, twenty-dollar cocktails and opt for domestic beer. One orders coq au vin. Can't go wrong with chicken. The other orders sweetbreads, feeling adventurous. Their waiter is charming and attentive and when their entrée takes thirty minutes to arrive, he brings them each a free glass of champagne, placing his index finger over his mouth. The food tastes even saltier than last time. It must be an off night for the chef from Cordon Bleu. They pass up dessert and settle for black coffee. This time they get out of there for under a hundred bucks.

Months later when they each receive a twenty percent discount coupon for treasured repeat customers, they decide to be optimistic and go once more. The outside fire pit is unlit as are all of the garden lights. The friends hesitate entering.

No one goes here anymore, a passing stranger says as they stare at the menu in the window.

Why not? they ask the stranger.

Because the food went down hill.

How do you know it went down hill?

That's what everyone is saying.

They are ravenous so they go in anyway. One dreary couple sits at a corner table. The Cordon Bleu chef and his family are at another. The friends order Niçoise salads and half a carafe of house red wine, which they discover is not included on the twenty percent special. Rather than dancing, the waiters seem to be carrying plates along as if they suddenly weighed twice as much. The wine tastes days old. Their jumpy, stooped waiter who is chewing gum is defensive. I just opened that bottle an hour ago, he says, and walks away from the table.

The empty bar looks sad and deserted, the paintings and teak floor dusty, the lighting harsh. When the salads arrive they are vinegary and limp. The maître d' seems ready to kill someone. As they rise to leave, he says, Come back and see us, as if it has taken all his breath to manage this farewell. Neither of our friends have the heart to tell him this will be their last visit.

A new restaurant they've just heard about is opening up around the corner. Everyone is talking about Volare! The chef is from Sicily and famous for his house-made Pasta con le Sarde and cannoli. Everything strictly authentic Italian cuisine. They don't take reservations. Our friends are thinking that if they get there a half hour before Volare! opens, they just might get lucky.

Saying Goodbye

We are in the last stretch of the sixth grade, just about to take the big leap to junior high school, with all its dark and delicious possibilities. On this rare drizzly June afternoon in otherwise sunny Los Angeles, Lynn and I run the several blocks from our elementary school to her house to watch our heroes do the Twist, the Pony and the Mashed Potato on American Bandstand. It's Friday, so freedom circulates in the air like confetti, and summer vacation is only a breath away.

With her sparkly ocean blue eyes and perfect beach tan, Lynn could be one of those girls on giant Pepsi billboards, beautiful girls who look so healthy, they make you believe Pepsi is good for you. I'm pretty too, but not in a spectacular way like Lynn, with practically every boy sick with love for her.

When we enter Lynn's front hallway, we can see past the living room into the den—one of those step-down, knotty pine add-ons with sliding glass doors looking out onto the backyard–where her parents are jumping up and down on the couch. From where we stand, her parents look small, like children or puppets. Their explosions of laughter remind me of the kids down at Trampoline Park on Pico Boulevard. Tirelessly jumping high in the air, falling down on their butts, and getting up again. Mr. and Mrs. Thorn seem like the wildest, most party-ish grown-ups alive, especially compared to my parents whose idea of fun is trying to guess the answers on "The Sixty-four Thousand Dollar Question."

Lynn yanks me back outside. "I just remembered our TV is broken. Let's go over to Patsy's. Her parents are in Hawaii, and she's got a giant Magnavox."

I want to ask her if her parents are celebrating something special. Why else would they both be home in the middle of the day? But she's already running down the street, so I take off after her, aware of the fact that we are missing the beginning of the show.

When we get to Patsy's, she's sitting on the floor eyes glued to the black and white TV screen. Dick Clark has just introduced a hit song by Paul Anka. It's a dreamy slow dance number, "Put Your Head On My Shoulder," and all the Bandstand regulars hook up with their partners on the dance floor. The audience's job is to judge the dance qualities of each song on a scale of zero to one hundred. We like to mimic the dancers as well as the judges.

Two at a time we dance close, pretending to be a girl and a boy, while the third girl judges the "romance factor." I pretend to be a boy kissing Patsy's neck and Lynn shrieks, "Bitchin'," and gives us a ninety. When Lynn bear hugs me and pushes her pelvis against my leg, I go into a musical trance, until Patsy howls with laughter. "Ninety-nine," she yells, "Give that couple a ninety-nine. They're totally in love!"

A year after the trampoline episode, we're in junior high school, and weighted down by algebra formulas and world history essays. Homework consumes our once lei-surely afternoons. Free time seems to belong to us less and less. The boys are still crazy about Lynn. They con-tinue to follow her around like lemmings, even though she's become moody and distracted ever since her par-ents' divorce.

"Do you miss your dad?" I ask one day as we walk home from school along the railroad tracks that run be-tween our houses. After hundreds of trips along these tracks, we've perfected our low-to-the-ground, tightrope walk–arms outstretched, feet gliding confidently along the narrow steel rails.

"Not really. It's better without him. My mom doesn't cry as much."

"What did she cry about?"

"Oh stuff, you know. Anyway, she doesn't anymore. Hey, I'm famished. Let's go raid my refrigerator," she says.

Usually we go to my house because my mother pro-vides a constant supply of Beverlywood Bakery pastries and half gallons of Rocky Road ice cream. I'm glad we're going to Lynn's today because I haven't seen Mrs. T. since the day she and Mr. T were jumping on the couch. I'm curious how she's doing without a husband.

When we arrive, we throw our books down in the hall and Lynn shouts out, "Hi Mom. I'm home. Annie's with me." We find Mrs. T sitting in the kitchen nook, elbows planted on the yellow Formica table. She's smoking a Camel and drinking Maxwell House instant black coffee out of a shallow, stained white cup.

"Hi girls," she says in her chronically hoarse voice, and continues to stare out the single window that frames the rusty swing set in her backyard. There are dark shadows under her blue eyes, and her wrists are as bony as our neighbor Mrs. Green's were before she died of leukemia. Mrs. Green left behind four little kids that according to my mother have become street urchins. When I see the pile of dishes in the sink, the empty cans of Jolly Green Giant corn and peas on the counter, I think Mrs. T. has become an urchin too.

Lynn wraps her arms around her mother and kisses the top of her head.

"Thanks honey," Mrs. T. says, then lifts her coffee cup to her lips and I see that her hands are shaking. Well, at least she's not crying.

Lynn makes us each a goopy peanut butter and jelly sandwich on Wonder Bread. We gobble them down while Mrs. T. smokes her cigarette down to the nub.

I've been friends with Lynn since second grade, and when we were little, Mrs. T. used to race to the door to greet us, literally bounce along on her tiny feet, giggling, then pick us up one at a time and twirl us around in the air. We'd follow her like puppies into the kitchen where it was warm and cozy and squeeze in beside her in the breakfast nook. Then she'd interview us like a talk show host, as if we were famous celebrities. "Lynn and Annie, our viewers want to know how the relay race went today. Was it terribly exciting? And did your teacher like the colorful map you drew of Africa?" Things like that. She made everything about our day seem special and important.

But today, she's on Mars. When the kettle whistles, she doesn't get up to shut it off. Lynn pops up and removes the kettle from the fire.

"Ricky Albertson wrote me a note today, Momma," she says. "He wants to meet me at the Picwood Theater on Saturday. Can I go?"

"He's the cutest and most popular boy at school," I add, hoping this good news will cheer up Mrs. T.

"We're almost out of milk," she says, still a planet away, her voice a low, raspy whisper, which I assume comes from inhaling too many unfiltered cigarettes. She doesn't answer about the movies, so I assume she's leaving the decision about meeting Ricky up to Lynn.

When Lynn reopens the refrigerator, I get a whiff of something rotting on the shelves. Boy, would my neatnik mother go nuts in this house, I think. No wonder Lynn's father moved out.

"Don't worry, Momma. There's still some left," Lynn smiles, holding up the milk carton and shaking it. "See?" She smiles triumphantly.

Just then Janice, Lynn's fourteen-year-old sister, comes into the kitchen wearing a faded yellow chenille bathrobe. Her eyelids are heavy, as if she's sleepwalking. She's come to fetch a Coke. Since Mr. T. left, Janice has become a weirdo even though she's pretty like Lynn. She used to have a bunch of friends and swam on the masters' team, but now she just hides out in her room. When I say hello to her at school, she looks like she doesn't recognize me even though I've slept over at Lynn's house a hundred times.

"Hi, Janice. How's it going?" I ask, as if she's perfectly normal.

"Okay." She yawns, cracking the bottle cap. Then without another word, she goes back to her room and shuts the door.

Lynn and I escape to her bedroom. Lynn stands in front of the full-length mirror, taking inventory of her figure from every angle while I do sit-ups on the shag rug. She has a slim waist and full breasts (unlike mine which are tiny things tucked into a training bra) and the curves of a Hollywood actress, unrivaled by any girl in our class. Her white-blonde hair is long, thick, and silky all the way down to her butt.

"You're so lucky," I say. "Ricky Albertson! Wow."

"My thighs are so fat," she says, her face crumbling in grief. "Totally gross."

"Maybe we should do Jack LaLanne," I joke.

By the time we're fifteen, Lynn has achieved her goal. She's gotten extra thin from smoking Marlboros and eating truckloads of celery stalks. She believes that the skinnier she gets the more beautiful she becomes and the more she will be loved. The boys seem to agree because they're wilder about her than ever.

Lynn and I invite boys over to my house when my parents are at work. We smoke cigarettes and drink beer the boys' older brothers buy for them. They hope to ply us girls with liquor so that they can score. We listen to the Beatles and Bob Dylan, which, along with the beer and our raging hormones, puts us in a reckless mood. We make out with the boys until our lips are swollen and bruised. Some of the boys' tongues dart around like lizards while others move slowly and seductively. They all wear tight white T-shirts and faded blue jeans and their nicotine mouths taste bitter, but their necks smell sweet-almost like girls' skin-drenched in Canoe. When we dance close I can feel the bulge in their pants as we press our bodies together. I feel powerful, and responsible for their erections.

After the boys go home, Lynn and I lie on my bed and gossip about kissing techniques. Sometimes we practice with each other as a way to improve and expand our make-out skills.

After a long, hot kiss that explodes into the giggles, Lynn says, "Gotta go. Mom needs me to help make dinner!" And she jumps up from the bed and rakes her fingers through her long silky hair.

"Is she okay?" I ask, astonished by the heat in my body.

"She's fantastic. Super busy, taking all sorts of classes at Santa Monica College. Hey Annie, okay with you if I take the leftover beer home with me?"

When we are sixteen, Lynn goes to stay with her Aunt Mary in Topanga Canyon, about twenty miles away. She doesn't tell the authorities she's changed addresses, and her Aunt Mary brings her down the mountain to school every day.

"It's cool up there, Annie. They have a horse I can ride any time I want. I feel so free!" Apparently, her mother got exhausted and had to go for a long rest at a secret retreat in Palm Springs. Lynn says the desert is curing her unhappiness. Meanwhile, her sister Janice has met some clunk-head surfer and is living with him in Malibu.

Fortunately, Topanga is close enough that Lynn and I get to see each other on weekends. Our friends with cars drive up into the canyon to pick her up, and then we all cruise the parties in Bel Air mansions where booze is in endless supply.

One night, while Lynn is making out with a stranger out by the pool, I drink too much sloe gin, which at first goes down like lemonade, but when I come home, I throw up on the front lawn.

In the morning, I'm hit hard by my first hangover and I call Lynn for advice. "I'm dying," I say.

"Take three aspirins and guzzle half a quart of orange juice," she says. "A sure cure for a hangover." She sounds almost happy that we are in the same predicament. After that, I stick to one or two beers, while Lynn experiments with wine, bourbon, and finally falls in love with vodka.

Boys still chase her, and without much difficulty, get her into the back seat of their cars. Sometimes after a particularly crazy weekend of partying, she says she can't remember whom she went home with the night before.

"Whoever it was, you won't hear from him again," I say in one of my bolder moments. "You're wasting your time with jerks who don't love you and are only out for sex."

"Oh Annie, you're just jealous," she replies and breaks into laughter. Maybe I am, I think, but not in the way she imagines.

Before too long, we're sitting in a dingy, back alley room in downtown L.A. Lynn has no idea who the father is and doesn't seem to care. She just wants to get the baby out of her. She and I have put together our babysitting money to pay for the abortion so Aunt Mary doesn't have to find out. I don't tell my mother either because I don't want to risk her telling Mrs. T.

As we sit in the waiting room, I can't think of anything to say, so from time to time I touch her shoulder or her bobbing knee. We're both shivering and Lynn's skin is tinged a sickly green color.

"Jeez, it's freezing in here," I finally say.

She doesn't answer. She just rocks her pale body back and forth, then pulls out a half pint of Smirnoff and takes a swallow.

"Maybe you shouldn't, before the thing," I say. "You know?"

"Oh, it's okay. I asked. They said it would help the pain."

"Oh."

"I'm so glad you're here," she says, squeezing my hand. "The best friend anyone could have. I don't deserve you, Annie," she says, and begins to cry. "I'd be better off dead."

"Don't talk like that," I say. "This will be over before you know it and everything will be back to normal." I smile reassuringly but I'm worried. What will I do if the doctor slips and Lynn bleeds to death? I'll be the one who has to tell Mrs. T. In True Confessions I read that they call this kind of back alley doctor a butcher. I imagine Lynn lying on the table with a wire hanger up her, blood dripping all over the floor. Just as I'm about to whisk her out of there, a scowling nurse comes into the waiting room and leads her away.

At the end of our senior year, we are seventeen and about to launch ourselves into the world. That's how our teachers and counselors describe our future. We are like rocket ships blasting off into the stratosphere. I've been accepted to U.C. Berkeley, and all my friends, including Patsy, will be attending four-year colleges in the fall, except Lynn, who's opted to work at Capezio shoe store until she figures out what she really wants to do. She's been too busy drinking and partying to keep up her grades or fill out applications for college.

Despite our differences, Lynn and I have stayed best friends for ten years, and kept our fantasies intact: She plans to come up to Berkeley to visit me, and I'll return to L.A. every few months to see her and my family. When we get married, we'll be each other's maid of honor. Eventually, we'll live next door to each other and raise our kids together. I try not to think about how practically everything we say to each other now is a lie. I've been crazy about her for as long as she's been crazy about alcohol.

Lynn calls me late at night, after her best and worst dates. She tells me about how much some new guy loves her, and then the next week she cries about how badly he's treated her. I listen patiently, then can't help but interject my opinions. "I told you that guy was an asshole." She always says I'm right. But the next night she'll be out with another loser, doing the same stupid shit.

On graduation day, after the ceremony, Lynn asks me to spend the afternoon with her.

"Just the two of us! We'll get royally blasted," she says, which is pretty much a daily thing for Lynn, but today she'll have my company.

"We can go to my house," she says. "My mom won't be there." Lynn moved back home when her mother returned from Palm Springs. "She's cured!" Lynn tells me. I don't ask why her mother, her father, her aunt, even her sister, don't show up for the graduation. I'm sick of watching Lynn strain to make up bullshit stories. No one recognizes a liar better than another liar.

Lynn has provided all the booze and mixers. I've brought chips and clam dip. We're sitting on the carpet in the den, reminiscing, rehashing embarrassing and thrilling moments that span the decade. It's amazing how old you can feel already at seventeen, like you have enough history to go on talking for days just about the past. And how complicated the truth has become–the parts of our lives that are easy to share, and the parts that remain hidden away. It's shocking how once lies get started, they pile up until you can't stop telling them, until they almost feel like the truth. I wonder if it is possible to grow up without becoming a liar.

We cover all the safe topics: teachers and students we have loved, envied and despised; the high and low points of our social lives; and our predictions of who we'll stay friends with and who we'll never see again.

The light is streaming through the sliding glass door and I look at the tattered, faded couch. It looks like furniture that's lived through the clawing and chewing of several feisty puppies, but the truth is, Lynn's family has never had a pet.

"Didn't Patsy look gorgeous?" Lynn asks, doing a forward bend on the rug, breasts to thighs. She's as limber as ever, only twenty pounds thinner.

"Yes, she did," I reply, stretching out beside her on the floor. "But she looked sad, too. It's a big deal, all of us separating."

"Yes, it's depressing. Everything's ending," she says, and pours a long shot of vodka into her glass, then a short pull of Rose's lime juice. "Oh Annie, we're not young anymore. We're old. And I have no fucking idea what I'm doing." She begins to cry and I put a comforting arm around her shoulder.

"You'll figure things out, Lynn. Remember that day, when we were kids and we came over here and found your parents jumping on the couch?"

"What about it?"

"They were just drunk. That was it, wasn't it?"

"I don't know. I can't remember," she says.

"They got divorced because of the drinking, didn't they?"

"Let's not talk about that shit, today. Today is happy-go-lucky day. You promised." She wipes the tears away and tries on a smile. "Nothing too morbid, okay?" She pours me a drink, hands it to me, and looks deeply into my eyes.

"You're the best, Annie."

"I love you too," I say, and swallow the entire drink.

In a short while we've got the stereo blasting the Stones' "I Can't Get No Satisfaction," and we're dancing around the room, alone, then with each other, sloppy and full of the giggles. Lynn's got a plastic rose between her teeth and I'm swirling a blanket in the air like a bull-fighter's cape, snapping my fingers, stamping my feet, getting crazy.

Lynn leaps all over the room, bumping the stereo, almost tipping over a lamp. Then she's on the couch, jumping higher and higher. "Come on, come on," she's yelling at me, pleading for me to join her. "I can't get no, can't get me no," her arms outstretched, fingers curling toward her palms, "sat-is-fac-tion!"

I pour myself another shot of vodka and gulp it down. My throat is on fire and within a couple minutes my limbs feel loose and free. I get on the couch, a little unsteady at first; then Lynn and I are holding hands, balancing each other, bouncing and falling together, getting up, reaching, reaching for something, then falling back down again. When our bodies collide, we become all tangled up together and our faces are dangerously close. I'm drunk in the way that makes you feel that everything you desire is possible. I lean in and kiss her full on the mouth. She quickly pulls away and looks startled.

"What are you doing?" she asks.

"Just practicing!" I joke, suddenly sober and terrified.

"Oh, Annie. You're such a card."

Then she reaches for the bottle and we each take another slug. I'm grateful for the numbness, and consider taking another swallow when she lifts herself up, and pulls me up with her. We're standing side by side on the lumpy old couch. Then we're jumping together again, singing and screaming along with Mick Jagger. Laughing and crying, jumping and collapsing on our butts, getting back up on our feet, over and over until we're both out of breath, exhausted, then jumping some more until it's out of our systems and we can say goodbye.

The Order of Things

Taking chances isn't my strong suit, unlike my twenty-three-year-old daughter, Brittany, who is all nerve and high risk. Who knows where that came from? The only risk her father ever took was cheating on me.

Currently, Brittany is working at Charles Schwab alongside her stockbroker boyfriend, Eric, learning all about hedge funds and leveraging, whatever they are. She constantly tells me I have to invest in my life, discover my passion, if I really want to live. She delivers the word "live" like it's jumping off a thirty-foot diving board.

This fall I was presented with the perfect opportunity to take a leap in my career. I am an intuitive and until now was practicing out of my San Francisco studio apartment, mostly trading with friends for reflexology and tarot readings.

My friend Penelope from book group told me about an affordable office available across the Golden Gate in a quaint brown-shingle in the heart of Wellfax, where she works as a massage therapist. The moment I walked into The Healing Arts Center, I could feel a vortex of power awaken at the center of my hara. Twenty-four hours later, I signed a two-year lease. The first person I called to share the good news with was Brittany.

"Congrats, Mom," she said, quickly informing me that Yelp is the lynchpin of a successful business. "You'll need to get five-star reviews," she instructed me. "Cards, flyers, eventually a website. It wouldn't hurt to blog and tweet. And don't forget to announce the opening of your practice on Facebook and Instagram." Though her techno advice was a bit overwhelming, I was determined to do what she suggested, at my own pace. I wanted her to be proud of me.

Until recently, being a mother had fulfilled me, but Brittany reminded me often enough that she was an adult now and I was free to explore other careers. In the Wellfax office, I would establish myself as a professional with a sliding scale and an embossed silver nameplate above my door. Even before I picked up the keys, I could feel an internal transformation occurring.

Since I was just starting out, I agreed to see a new client on a Friday at 9:00 P.M. I couldn't be too picky about my hours, especially in my profession–services that many people see as a luxury rather than a necessity. Also, I had just dished out a hefty first and last month's rent and wanted to make some of that money back sooner than later. Nine o'clock was the earliest Marcy, a recent breast cancer survivor and full-time checker at Safeway, could come. Even though I was battling a sinus headache, I looked forward to my session with her. I prepared myself by doing a series of grounding exercises. Then I smudged the room with sage, lit mandarin orange-scented votives, cleared my chakras, and took a few bites of my kale and quinoa salad.

When I heard the Tibetan bells hanging on my door begin to chime, I sprayed grapefruit oil mist into the air to absorb toxins and create an uplifting atmosphere. Since we already knew each other from Spirit Crossing, the nearby Buddhist Meditation Center, it seemed natural and appropriate to greet Marcy with a sisterly hug. One night recently, at Spirit Crossing, after an inspiring talk on "Conscious Forgiveness in the New Millenium," Marcy and I had chatted about "letting go" while at the tea table. Despite her health crisis, her smile was radiant. I admired her positive attitude under such duress. Before we parted that night, she asked for my card, which luckily I had picked up at the printer's that afternoon.

I pointed to her chair, and sat down directly across from her in mine. First, we made meaningful eye contact; then, together, we closed our eyes and took several deep cleansing breaths. As soon as I went into trance, Marcy's deceased mother, grandmother, and golden retriever Buddy visited us in spirit form. Then I received a powerful transmission regarding Marcy's current health status. Gazing deeply into her green eyes, I said, "My guides are telling me that you are cancer-free, and that a growing closeness with your teenaged son is on the horizon."

"How did you know about my son?" She looked ecstatic.

"These messages just come through me," I told her. "I am merely a conduit." Since childhood, I have channeled the hidden and the unexpected. Marcy couldn't have been happier with the reading. Her dewy eyes and flushed complexion told me everything.

"Blessings," I said and clasped her hands.

"Blessings," she repeated. "Thank you. Thank you." And then she squeezed my hands with astonishing force.

I felt white light traveling through my body and into my extremities. Words were unnecessary. We were communicating on the astral, which I find far more satisfying than normal conversation. I was certain Marcy would be back.

When she left, I collected her used Kleenex and threw them into the wastebasket; I blew out the citrus-scented candles and tamped down the amber incense. Reviewing my reading, I decided it had been one of my best. Working in an office rather than at home had heightened my vibration. The wisdom of the universe streamed effortlessly through me as my spiritual guide, Ajante, sat on my shoulder like a magnificent winged bird.

I felt confident that I would build a thriving practice in my new green, eco-friendly location, drawing simpatico people like Marcy into my practice and accumulating an impressive number of five-star Yelp reviews. No more hiding away in my dark San Francisco apartment eating Chinese-to-go and enduring debilitating migraines. I would live! Wellfax's darling neighborhood cafes provided a perfect venue for striking up lively conversation with like-minded people. And, perhaps, I thought, I will finally meet a heterosexual man with spiritual sensitivities aligned with my own.

When I bent down to straighten the tassels of the red and blue Tibetan rug, I felt a sudden urgency, and ran to the bathroom, unconsciously shutting the door behind me. When I returned, I discovered my office door was locked! My sense of well-being popped as jarringly as a balloon pricked by a pin.

It was after ten o'clock and I was locked out of my new office! All the other practitioners were long gone. I jiggled the doorknob and it refused to budge. I was stranded with no wallet, no keys, no cell phone, no money, nada. My first thought was to phone Brittany who has a key to my apartment. She and Eric live only blocks from my studio where I hid my spare office key in a hand-woven basket on top of the fridge. Though I try not to disturb the lovebirds, the idea of wasting a hundred dollars on cab fare for a forty-minute ride, or a locksmith was unacceptable to me, especially after having just forked up the money for rent as well as office furniture and paint. My sign wasn't up yet. No one knew me. Inconveniently, my new landlord was wine tasting in Provence, and Penelope, my only friend in town, was visiting her sickly mother in San Diego. I was stranded except for Brittany.

I recalled that the Pizza Palace across the street stayed open late. I explained my predicament to the proprietor who let me use his phone.

"May all blessings fill your life," I said, looking deeply into his kind grey eyes.

"Brittany, it's me, Mom. Don't worry," was the first thing I said. She hates it when I get "emotional." Thankfully the voicemail memory wasn't full, which it often is. "Well... I accidentally locked myself out of my office. It was a long day and I guess I was tired. Anyway, could you possibly bring me the spare key? It's in the small basket I bought at the Indian market in Taos. I'll wait here to hear from you. I'm at the Pizza Palace across the street. 415-823-3102. Okay. I'm so sorry."

I waited for half an hour, drinking ice water and staring intermittently at the crumbling oil-stained wallpaper and the blinking Budweiser clock. I felt self-conscious not ordering anything and began to wonder if I had left the incense burning on my altar. I tried to reassure myself that even if I had, it would eventually burn itself out. Then, to further calm my disrupted energy body, I focused intensely on my Emotional Freedom Technique, diligently tapping the appropriate release points on my body.

"Even though I locked myself out of the office, I totally and completely accept myself."
I tapped the karate chop side of my hand and then moved on to my eyebrows.
"Even though I am a stupid fucking idiot, I totally and completely accept myself."
I tapped the sides of my eyes and under my nose.
"Even though my mother never nurtured me or taught me how to thrive in the world, I totally and completely accept myself."
I tapped under my lip and moved down to my collarbone.

When Brittany didn't call back, I assumed that she had temporarily turned off her cell while having sex with Eric. I employed a variety of additional clearing techniques, even entertained the idea of paying the outrageous hundred bucks for a cab, but then I realized I still wouldn't have the key to my apartment. I was trapped. So I swallowed my pride and asked the shy, grey-eyed stranger for permission to use his phone again. He nodded approval then scooted a large pepperoni pizza into the red-hot brick oven.

"It's Mom again. Listen. I'm starting to feel weird hanging out here, so I'm going to return to my office.

Great. I'll wait for you in the vestibule. Hope you get this message soon." Of course, I assumed she'd check her messages; like the rest of her generation, Brittany is electronically hooked up 24/7. She is as addicted to her iPhone as she is to sex.

Back at the building, I noticed that I had inadvertently left a small window open in my office. Perhaps I could climb through and handle this mess myself! Wouldn't it be glorious to phone Brittany back and say, "No worries. I climbed a wall and dove through the window. Problem solved."

Stepping onto a wobbly log, I braced myself against the outside wooden wall, gripped the ledge, and tried to boost myself up by my arms. At the moment, I deeply regretted not taking Pilates or Zumba or keeping up my sun salutations.

Too close to the shingles, I tore the lace on the hem of my dress, then bumped my head on the windowsill. "Shit," I blurted. My energy field was emitting intense negativity. Lilith, I told myself, this is one of those opportunities when Ajante would say, "Galvanize the Goddess within."

I tried a few more times to angle my body through the tiny window, but I kept getting stuck at the hips and sliding back down to the ground. Accepting defeat, I returned to the vestibule where the room temperature wasn't any warmer than the outside air. The thermostat was set to an automatic timer, and there was no way to engage it after 10:00 P.M. There were two stiff-back chairs, a lumpy couch and a magazine rack.

Pacing the floor, my mind spit out hypotheses. Perhaps Brittany had picked up my first message and was on her way. Maybe I should return to the Pizza Palace. No, she'd come here as soon as she got my second message. But what if she was still lounging in bed with Eric, riding post-coital waves of bliss, temporarily detached from her iPhone?

Modern technology has made communication unnecessarily complicated and confusing. In the old days, you dialed someone on your clunky black telephone and the person either picked up or they didn't. You knew when you had reached someone. But these days a caller can obsess about a delivered message: "Did she or he receive my voicemail, email, text? Was I in or out of range? Are they online, offline, screening their calls, avoiding me, out of the country, dead?"

For all I knew, Brittany was just as likely sound asleep as speeding to my rescue. She might have run into traffic or an accident on the Golden Gate Bridge, and, of course, would be unable to inform me. Everything was pure speculation.

To root myself to the earth, I placed one hand against the vestibule wall and managed a shaky tree pose, then followed with an extended forward bend. I let the blood rush to my head. "Trust," I heard Ajante whisper in my ear, "Everything is evolving as it should. Be here now." She loved combining her messages with Ram Dass's. It was as if I had received a double transfusion of confidence. My heart swelled with luminescence. Despite my present hardship, I would prevail.

Sitting on the lumpy blue couch in the vestibule, I thumbed through *Health Magazine*, then the latest *Yoga Journal*, marveling at the photos of inverted poses I was too afraid to attempt myself. Another hour passed while I tried to imagine a forgivable reason why Brittany hadn't come to retrieve me. I know what you're thinking. "Call the fucking locksmith!"

Looking back now, I can clearly see that would have been the right decision. But in my defense, I had lost connection to both reason and spirit. The kind of breakdown that leads to cerebral disequilibrium. To be honest, I had probably regressed to about the age of six. Emotionally kicking and screaming, I wanted Brittany to be the grown-up and rescue me. Foolishly, I trounced back across the street to phone her one last time.

The gentle proprietor was now washing wine glasses in the nearly empty restaurant. I told him the reason I was being such a pest was that I had just moved into an office in the medical building across the street and was locked out. "It's embarrassing to appear so needy at our first encounter." I laughed.

"No problem," he waved his hand in the air as if to say, I know you are much more than you seem.

"Brittany, it's me again. The pizza place is closing. And I have no intention of going into one of the dive bars to call you again. This is no joke. I'm stranded." I almost said, "you little spoiled bitch." "I know you were just here on Tuesday to help me paint, but there's nothing I can do about the lousy timing!" I managed to hang up before I started to cry.

Once again, I heard Ajante's voice encouraging me. "Lillith, empower yourself! Think in different categories," another borrowed phrase. So, I opened the yellow pages and searched for a local locksmith. I reached Murphy's 24-hour Reliable Locks and Keys. Tom Murphy seemed qualified and nice enough until he quoted me his minimum fee of $185. I was shocked and told him so. He made it clear that his nighttime rate was firm. I thanked him, and hung up. He may have been reliable, but he was also a crook.

Currently, Brittany and Eric were living the good life in Eric's recently purchased high-end condo, which came with a doorman, Enrique, who they treat like a first cousin. Enrique this and Enrique that. Eric thought nothing of dropping $200 on a late-night supper downtown or $50 on a bottle of wine, but not before he consulted Zagat's. Food, money and sex were his best friends. And I was afraid he had reinforced Brittany's own sense of entitlement as well as her tendency to value the material above the spiritual.

Until she was nine, Brittany and I were inseparable. While Ronald built houses and remodeled kitchens, she sat on my lap and played with my hair. On sunny days, we strolled hand in hand to Stowe Lake to feed the ducks or dodged waves at Baker's Beach. On our returns from the library, we splurged on double scoops of chocolate ice cream at Bud's. Wherever we went, we pointed out the magic we saw, like rainbows in puddles, and tiny plants shooting up through the sidewalk.

When she was eleven, she briefly joined me in my love of the occult and we frequently threw the I Ching and consulted the Ouija board for guidance. We also redecorated the house together, using the principles of feng shui. We were more than mother and daughter. We were best friends.

I divorced Ronald when she was thirteen. After that I had to fight him for every cent Brittany needed for private school, flute lessons, and tennis camp. I've tried to make up for the divorce by providing my daughter with adventures I missed out on in my youth. I wanted to give Brittany everything my parents couldn't afford.

After her father moved out, Brittany shut herself in her room with her Apple earphones. Sometimes it was so quiet in there; it was as if she was in a coma. Then suddenly, she'd burst out of her room and throw a tantrum because we were out of yogurt or because I was playing Joni Mitchell too loudly.

She wasn't herself, or let's say she was the newly invented, hormonally imbalanced, uncommunicative Princess Brittany. For days she'd refuse to say good morning to me. Then out of the blue, she'd run into my arms and squeeze me so tight I could hardly breathe. Her moods were brutal. After one eighteen-hour silent marathon, I knocked on her door and she shrieked, "Mom, I need space! You should get a dog!" With Penelope's prompting, I signed up for classes at the Institute for Intuitive Studies. I had to find another way to be in this world. Everyone I knew agreed I was clairvoyant. That was the beginning of my career as a psychic.

Last summer, before she hooked up with Eric, Brittany came home for a few months to save money and leech off the built-in chef and laundress. During one of our heated arguments over who was going to recycle, she screamed, "No wonder you and Daddy split up. You'd drive anyone fucking nuts."

"Brittany, you cannot talk to me that way." I was so angry I came close to slapping her; instead, I visualized sending energy down through the roots of my feet into the earth. I said, "I'm going out for a while and when I get back we'll discuss everything calmly."

I drove around the block several times. I looked up at the stars and thought about how Brittany acted as if she were the center of the universe, and how Ronald swore her selfishness was my fault. Maybe he was right. When I returned she was heating up leftover Thai food and had set the table for two. That was an encouraging moment for me, and I think for her as well.

In all fairness, Brittany didn't have it easy as a kid. For thirteen years, she was a witness to my fights with Ronald and when it was revealed that he was having an affair, she got furious at him, then turned on me, accusing me of being a cold fish. "Brittany! He slept with half my friends," I told her, and "when we tried to make love he was always impotent." I know I involved her too much in the details of my marriage, and that I shouldn't have bad-mouthed her father, even though he is a complete asshole.

I had dozed off on the hard velvet couch, the Yoga Journal on my face. I looked up at the wall clock and was surprised to see it was 3:30. I was shivering with cold, my fingertips blanched white. I clenched and unclenched my fists to get the blood flowing. Standing, I jumped up and down in place, but my back was stiff and I was afraid I'd throw it out. I felt awkward and foolish, like an arthritic pretending to be a pole-vaulter. Stretching my arms overhead, I swayed from side to side, praying to the heavens for guidance. The increased oxygen circulating in my brain fired up more feelings.

Brittany is almost twenty-four, I thought. Older than I was when I married Ronald. It's time she gave something back. Everything isn't about her. It's no longer my job to make her happy. My job is to make myself happy. "She's not coming," I said aloud and began to cry. "The bitch isn't coming."

Allowing myself this moment of self-pity, I faced the unbearable revelation that the idealized equation I'd had in my head forever wasn't going to work out as planned. Brittany wasn't going to give me what I had given her. It just wasn't in the order of things. While standing half frozen and isolated in a dark waiting room with no phone, no money, no partner, and a tenuous profession, I breathed in the truth: I was alone in the world.

Looking back, $185 for a locksmith would have been nothing compared to this night of torture. It was four o'clock now and nothing was open, not even the dive bars. Not a soul roamed the streets with a cell phone, so I couldn't have called anyone even if I knew who to call. By five, I was so tired and cold, I couldn't think, and had lost all sense of hope. My feet were ice, my nose numb to the touch. All I wanted was a warm bed to sleep in.

At some point I had to pee again, so I drudged upstairs to use the bathroom. It was locked! Had I done this too? "What the fuck is going on? Was this duca? Where did all my good karma go?" Frantic, I ducked outside into the bushes at the side of the building. The streets were empty and bathed in deep shades of black, but I squatted down low anyway behind a tree fern. Mid-stream, an animal sprinted from behind an oak and startled me. I looked into its cocky bandit eyes. A raccoon. Instinctively, I pulled up my underpants and ran back inside before I could air dry.

I folded myself into a tight package on the couch and waited for the cleaning people to arrive at 8:00 A.M.

Lying in the dim light, barely moving, not having eaten for hours, feeling physically weak and emotionally spent, I didn't know what to think about Brittany

anymore. Apathy invaded me, offering a strange, sur-
real relief, as if I were suddenly very far away from my
own body and feelings. As well as I thought I knew my
daughter, at the moment, she was a complete mystery to
me. All people are mysteries to one another. Even one's
children. Especially one's children. There was nothing a
parent could do but let go and see what happens next–
another of Adjante's favorite refrains. Even as a devoted,
spiritually informed person, "letting go" was an excruciating task for me.

When a sliver of morning sunlight filtered into the
waiting room, I looked outside to the brightening blue
skies. As the sun began to warm my cheeks, I smelled hon-
eysuckle and heard chirping birds flit about outside. And
then I heard Ajante's voice stronger than ever: "Pay attention to the wisdom of impermanence." The universe was
showering me with gifts. I had survived the cold night,
endured the darkness, and was stronger for it. And now,
the day was delivering its warmth and light. My faith in
the natural cycles of life was restored. My heart softened
toward myself and toward all beings everywhere.

At 7:15, two cheerful women in their twenties, wearing shorts and tennis shoes, bounded into the vestibule,
interrupting my daydream. They were like a burst of sun-
shine; I untwisted my body in their direction and squinted up at them.

They told me they were on their way to Point Reyes
for a hike and had stopped by to pick up a trail map one of
my suitemates had left for them on the communal coffee
table. I smiled, and asked if one of them had a cell phone
I could borrow to call my daughter.

"Of course," the one called Jane said.

This time Brittany picked up. Hearing her real voice startled me. "Why didn't you come get me?" I blurted.

"I just picked up your messages. I was so exhausted last night, I turned off my cell."

"Turned it off? Why would you turn it off?"

"You're the one who's always saying I'm too addicted to it! Anyway, do you want me to come now?"

"Now? No, not now. It's too late. I mean, I'll be fine. I am fine." And though I was half pretending, part of me believed it was true. "Two nice women just arrived here and are keeping me company. The cleaning people will be here any minute with the keys. Then I'm going home to sleep! I'll talk to you later," and for the first time in my life, I hung up on my daughter.

I looked up at the two hikers who were staring back at me with concern. They asked what was wrong, and I poured out my story. The tears just came. They each placed a compassionate hand on my shoulder, listening attentively while I spoke and wept. Then the one called Delia offered to go get us all coffee and scones at the local drive-by hut. While Delia was gone, Jane and I talked openly and honestly about the challenges between mothers and daughters.

When Delia returned with the coffee and berry scones, we all sat together on the couch and chatted–they insisted on staying with me until I was safely in my office. When the cleaning crew arrived, I thanked Jane and Delia for their generosity. "You are very dear." It was their pleasure, they said. What sweet, healing words. Their pleasure! Just then I wished they could be my children, my better daughters, and I could say, nonchalantly, "After your hike, why not come for lunch? I'll make fattoush salads and afterward, we can load up on chocolate ice cream!" But I heard Ajante's voice loud and clear. "Time to move on, Lilith."

So I said, "May all blessings fill your life," and we all hugged goodbye like family. When they were gone, I entered my office, gathered up my belongings, and checked my cell phone messages. Well, what do you know? A new client referred by Marcy! Definitely a sign! I called her immediately and set up an appointment for the following day at 10:00 A.M., a respectable time of day. No more working at night for me. I had learned my lesson. One door closes as another one opens.

Namaste, Ajante.

The Hoarder

R etirement Hotel, Oakland California
April 15, 2012

When my father died a decade ago, my fiercely independent mother, then a spry eighty-four-year-old, insisted on remaining in their Los Angeles hillside home,
alone. It wasn't until she slipped and broke her femur in
seven places that my sister and I convinced her to move
up north near us. For the past nine years, she has lived
in a retirement hotel in Oakland where she uses a stur-
dy walker to cross the street to a local strip mall that
includes a CVS, Safeway, Lucky Dry Cleaners, Happy
Nails, and Starbucks. Early on, her single destination
was Starbucks where she drank a $2.95 steamy mocha
with extra whipped cream every morning. Surrounded
by people working at their laptops, she felt young again,
a part of things. A few doors down from Starbucks, she
soon discovered The Dress Barn, and it was as if a barn

door had opened onto a field of fashion. After fifty-six years of living with her coupon-collecting husband, my mother suddenly realized that all the money was now hers and she could spend it however the hell she pleased. She quickly became a favorite customer of The Dress Barn's twenty-something saleswomen who admired her thick, snow-white hair, erect posture, incomparable spunk, and uncanny willingness to use her credit card every day.

"You are a natural beauty," they said. "Everything you try on looks terrific."

My mother trusted these professional flatterers, and whenever she skipped a day or two, they reported missing her terribly. At first she bought one modest item at a time–a blouse, a pair of slacks–each one a special treat, a widow's right. Then she graduated to pants suits with coordinated shells; sweaters and shirts in colors to match her mood; imitation Tiffany bangles, polyester scarves; and eventually, duplicates of the clothing she'd purchased only days before. At least when it came to purchasing bulk items on sale at CVS and Safeway, my father's frugality still reigned. She bought jumbo packs of everything. It was not unusual to discover her cabinets crammed with so much Crest, Ajax, Star-Kist tuna, and Charmin Ultra Soft, my sister and I ended up doing our weekly shopping at her tiny studio apartment. Sometimes I needed sponges while my sister had just run out of Shout. We divided up mint-flavored dental floss, Lady Schick razors and Eveready batteries. We joked about opening a family thrift store that would give Mom something to do other than shop compulsively.

"Take this home," she encouraged us. "I have too many." She loved giving us practical gifts.

Over time, we began to notice Mom's purchases made less and less sense: thirty lipsticks in shades from pale pink to fire-engine red; party-size bags of Doritos and Reese's Pieces; pots of geraniums, lucky bamboo; a stuffed toy kangaroo, Minnie Mouse, and a devil with a red cape lined up on the bed like an army of protectors. There were wooden plaques with such corny sayings as "When life gives you lemons, make lemonade."

Whenever we expressed concern about depleting reserves, she would say, "I have plenty of money," and change the subject.

This was the not the mother I grew up with. When I was a kid my mother was a neatnik. Every object in our house had its place, and Mom took pride in her dust-free home. Now, when my sister and I tripped over the accumulation of newspapers, magazines, and decorative pillows in her living room, we felt we had no choice but to consult a therapist. Hoarding, we learned, was one of the hardest addictions to break. In the elderly it often serves as a defense against dying, so the therapist said we shouldn't expect to stop or curtail my mother's spending. Essentially, this counselor invited us to "let go."

One drizzly Saturday afternoon, Mom purchased a three-foot-tall brass plant stand, balanced it on the seat of her walker, carted it across the busy crosswalk, pushed it into the elevator in her building, and finally, set it in a corner of her overcrowded apartment. For a ninety-four year-old, this was equivalent to Phillippe Petit's 1974 tightrope walk between the Twin Towers.

When I dropped by that evening, the stand was loaded with plants.

"Do you love it?" I asked with a forced smile, practicing letting go.

"Not really," she answered, adjusting her faux CVS pearls in the mirror. Then she reached for her purse.

"Come," she said, directing her walker toward the hall. "Let's eat out. My treat."

For weeks after consulting the therapist about my mother's hoarding, I tried to look the other way when I noticed new items atop her refrigerator, or old ones relegated to the balcony: the dried-up plants; topless lipsticks coated with sunflower seeds and lint; the rain-soaked kangaroo now missing a leg and an ear. Soon enough, her monthly credit card bill had tripled, and my letting-go policy went out the window along with my patience. Friends assured me I needed to intervene.

"You need to think of yourself as the CEO of a company that is going down fast," one of them told me.

I decided on a plan, and a few days later found Mom in an egg-stained bathrobe, looking especially vulnerable without makeup. On her coffee table were half a dozen empty picture frames in which she planned to put family photos. She complained that there was no more room on the walls or dresser to show them off.

"I've gone a little bit crazy, haven't I?" she said, looking like a little girl. "I keep buying things. I never used to do that. All I want is to have Daddy back."

"I understand," I said, pushing my chair a bit closer to hers. "I know." Then I looked into her eyes. "Do you think it would be better, Mom, if I held onto your credit card for a while? We could set it aside for special, fun occasions. Meanwhile, I could bring you money each week for everyday expenses."

To my amazement, she simply said, "Yes." In her eyes, I saw nothing but relief. She handed over the credit card and I withdrew several twenty-dollar bills from my wallet.

"You are a wonderful girl," she said. "I did good."

"Thanks, Mom," I said, and hugged her. On the way out, I grabbed a box of Kleenex decorated with butterflies and a handful of Reese's Pieces.

Footface

After I broke my big right toe, it hurt so badly that one night I chopped it off with an axe and within days, it healed and began to grow back. Instead of an oblong shape, a round ball appeared at the end of my foot. Before long, the little ball became a head with a face that sprouted features. First two ears popped out, followed by two eyes and a nose. The mouth was the last to appear and when it did, it said, "Hello there!"

Stunned, I answered, "Who are you?"

"I love you," it said, and smiled.

Gazing at the tiny head that had replaced my toe, I tried to figure out whom it looked like. There was a little of my mother in the dark eyes and high cheekbones. The nose actually resembled my childhood dog, Scout. Still it was its own unique face, and frankly, one I found rather unattractive. I felt guilty about feeling this way since Footface was showing me so much affection. "I don't care where we go," it repeated often. "I just like being with you."

While performing a forward bend in yoga class, I stared at the drooping eyelids and accumulation of wrinkles around its eyes and mouth, characteristics that made the little face seem tired and old. My reaction troubled me so I went to see my therapist.

"I want to love Footface," I whispered to Dr. Boyd, "but I'm having trouble accepting its appearance."

Dr. Boyd asked, "Is that because she looks like you?"

"Me?" I said, horrified. "Is that what I look like?"

My therapist handed me a mirror and I saw that in fact Footface was my miniature twin. And she was clearly a girl.

Dr. Boyd suggested I practice empathy. "How does Footface feel when people gawk at her when you stroll downtown in your flip-flops?"

"It makes me want to hide under a table," Footface piped up.

"Sometimes, I feel that way too," I said.

"She is you and you are she, and we are all one," Dr. Boyd said with her eyes closed. After her spiritual invocation, I looked down and saw that Footface was smiling beatifically. Taking her to therapy had been an elixir.

After that session, we entered a state of grace. I took Footface shopping at Toys R Us and bought her doll-size clip-on earrings, then onto Aveda for a sample-size volumizing mousse for her hair, which had been growing an inch a week. With my cuticle scissors I created a stylish Annie Lennox do that kept her hair from dragging along the floor and collecting dust. In the spring, I surprised her with a "Let's Get Pink" lipstick from Macy's along with an SPF15 facial moisturizer and bronzer. She glowed when she said, "Thanks for the makeover!"

Footface

When she developed weed and tree allergies, I fed her microchips of Claritin. And in the nippy fall, I covered her head with a woolen cap that I crocheted over a thimble.

"What would I do without you?" she cooed.

We became closer each day, sharing laughs over silly everyday things like where had I left my reading glasses or car keys this time! We took hundreds of selfies at home, at the beach, and in cafes, which we posted on Facebook, receiving 983 likes in seven minutes. Sometimes I looked at her while she slept, and thought, she is quite beautiful.

Then one night while I watched "Grey's Anatomy" on Netflix and munched popcorn, Footface blurted, "Do you really want all that butter? You've put on weight lately, and believe me, I can feel it." I did not appreciate her observation. Yet, shortly thereafter, I took up jogging in my Tevas, and right away Footface complained about the impact of the pavement. So I switched to the mountain trails, but then she yelled, "You're throwing dirt in my face." I just couldn't please her. Disgruntled, I turned my attention elsewhere.

A friend introduced me to a Sarah Lawrence girl who I met at a local bar for gin and tonics. We were having a lively conversation about Sylvia Plath's poem "Cut," and I could feel the chemistry between us, but Footface kept twitching. When the lit major went to the bathroom, Footface screamed, "Let's go! It's stuffy in here and besides, she's a bitch." When Sarah Lawrence returned she found me arguing with my toe, and said she had to leave. That night Footface had bad dreams. She tossed and turned all night, giving me Restless Leg Syndrome.

After several months of bickering, I shouted at Foot-face, "Shut up! I need quiet time to read Middlemarch. You must respect my love for the classics!"

She went mute, but within five minutes began chattering again, this time about her strained relationship with my other nine toes. "They treat me like a pariah," she whined. Things got worse when I went for a pedicure. Footface went into a jealous rage and I had to calm her down with several shots of Don Julio.

I had the urge to chop her off, but had a hunch that she might grow back as one of the Kardashians.

I returned to my therapist.

"Footface is driving me nuts," I told her. "We just don't get along."

Dr. Boyd said I had more work to do. If I could learn to accept myself, I would be able to accept Footface. I argued that until Footface came along, I had accepted myself, unconditionally.

"And yet you did chop off your toe with an axe," she said, non-judgmentally.

"True," I said, beginning to doubt that I had ever really loved and accepted myself, or anyone else for that matter. Maybe my whole life was a sham. "Tell me Dr. Boyd, what can I do to heal?"

"For starters, we should ask Footface what she needs." Just then, Footface fell off and rolled across the carpet. Dr. Boyd and I knelt beside her to see if she was okay.

"I need space," she announced, sounding very independent.

"What did I do wrong?" I began to cry.

"Nothing," Dr. Boyd reassured me. "She's just individuating. Have faith. For now, perhaps you should both come in three times a week."

We all agreed to the new schedule. Then Dr. Boyd and I hugged before I hobbled out with Footface rolling along beside me.

Girls Gone Astray

I t was a hot Friday afternoon in September of 1997 in Marin County. A real scorcher, and as usual, Cat and I walked home together after a grueling soccer practice. Our houses were blocks apart, and she was planning to stay for dinner. She never invited me to her house. I figured it was because her family had eight kids and their house was probably a disaster.

After dinner, Cat and I took Zeplin, our hard-breathing bulldog, for his evening walk.

"Zep has a deviated septum. That's why he snores louder than my father," I told Cat, and she cracked up. She often told me how funny I was, which made me feel amazing. She was such a sweet and gorgeous girl.

We circled the nearby park and then met up with other seniors from our high school. One guy named Trent passed a joint around. Everyone took a hit, except Cat. She said she preferred a contact high. We all watched the stars twitch in the sky while smoke tendrils drifted from our mouths. It was easy to lose track of time as the hard edges of our athletic bodies blurred and disappeared in the darkness.

When we returned home, my mom stood barefoot in the yard in her tank top and shorts, hair piled recklessly on top of her head. She was soaking the plants because the following day was predicted to be another sizzler. Inside, my dad was slouched on the couch in his boxers reading about amalgams. He's a dentist who works hard prowling around in people's mouths searching for decay. My mother is a pediatric nurse at Kaiser who loves her job, and loves going out after work with her nurse girl-friends to play pool and drink gin and tonics.

On this night, she looked exceptionally happy and content as she watered the thirsty plants. I think she liked these dark, quiet hours alone when Dad fell out on the couch and read about teeth. Mom and Dad had been married for over twenty years and I knew they loved each other in a solid way, but it seemed like the romance had worn off. I wanted to fall madly in love and stay that way until my last breath.

After we said goodnight to my parents, Cat and I hung out on the twin beds in my bedroom in our tanks and bikini underpants. These 100-degree days barely dropped below 80 at night, so we surfed the net with the covers off. I checked my emails and Cat wrote a handwritten letter to her cousin Macy in Utah. I got a full-of-herself email from my sister, Olivia, a freshman at NYU, in which she described her life-changing encoun-ters in Soho, listing all the boys-she called them men- she was having sex with. I was writing her back when Cat cried out.

"What happened?" I bolted upright.

"Something bit me," she said.

I leapt out of bed and ran to her. "Where? Let me see." "Here" she put my hand on the spot and I felt a hot bump rising on her neck. "Wow. That's huge. Maybe it's a spider bite," I said. "Should I get the calamine lotion?"

"No, I'm good," she said and kissed my cheek. "Thanks." Then she stared into my eyes with such intensity I finally broke the spell with nervous laughter.

My mother knocked on the door. "Goodnight girls," she said. Both our bodies went rigid as sticks. Cat announced that she was tired and quickly turned over to sleep. "Yeah, me too," I said, even though I could have stayed awake all night. I returned to my own bed, wondering if Cat was thinking what I was thinking, which was the unthinkable.

I was planning to apply to Columbia to major in psychology the following year and room with my sister on Bleeker Street. I couldn't wait to get out of Marin, out of the trees and into the happening city life of Manhattan. I was glad I hadn't gotten attached to any particular boy. Now unexpectedly, I was obsessed with a hometown girl who wanted to attend UC Davis to become a veterinarian.

Indian summer continued to assault us. Cat and I liked to hang out in the shady redwood grove at school. We sat side by side on an uncomfortable wooden bench carved up with the initials of lovers, current and long-gone. We didn't mention what happened in my bedroom but I felt intoxicated around her now, riveted to her exotic blue eyes and irresistible smile. I'd kissed my fair share of boys but nothing had impacted my physiology like this. I couldn't believe that a single look from Cat had created a desire in me so large it now ruled my life. At night I took my fantasies into the stratosphere working myself into a frenzied exhaustion. Had I lost my mind?

I thought about the recent puppy episode on The Ellen Show and how Ellen's TV character came out to Laura Dern. And then the real Ellen DeGeneres came out on Oprah! The whole world knew. I admired Ellen's courage to be completely honest about who she was, and it made me feel better about who I might be becoming.

One day while we ate our lunch in the grove, Cat clutched my wrist as she took a bite of my apple. That was all the encouragement I needed.

I leaned in for a kiss just as Billy Peters, a kid whose face was covered with eczema, walked by. "Hey, you better watch out. If Jasper catches you, you'll be suspended." Miss Jasper was our scary principal, known for her vindictive, harsh punishments.

"We're just having lunch," I shouted. "It's a free world."

Cat elbowed me. "Hey, Billy. How's it going?"

"Okay," he said, scowling, and he walked away.

"He's weird," I said.

Cat stiffened. "We should be nice to outsiders like Billy because he suffers. Just like us."

"What do you mean? I'm not suffering."

"Everyone suffers," she said.

"You're right," I said to keep the peace.

Full of longing, I convinced Cat to meet me after school behind the bungalows at the far end of campus. "No one ever goes there. I want to talk to you about something," I said, even though I couldn't imagine what I was going to say.

I waited behind the decrepit wooden shack, my heart racing. Closing my eyes, I listened to the light-hearted laughter of kids funneling through the school gate. I thought I heard some of my friends' exuberant voices–Mattie, Royce and Emily. Would they be creeped out if I told them I had a crush on a girl? Were there other students who were in hiding or were Cat and I the only ones?

When the last of the students' voices faded, I peeked around the corner searching for Cat. Every minute that passed was like an hour. My stomach tightened. My brain buzzed. Maybe I'd misread the signals or scared her away. Maybe I wasn't pretty or clever enough, or worth the risk.

And then a soccer ball came speeding my way. Cat had kicked it and she was standing a few feet in front of me smiling mischievously.

"Our cover," she said.

When we kissed for the first time, my stomach did crazy heart-stopping acrobatics.

"Wow," I said.

"Are we being really bad?" she asked innocently.

"We're not hurting anyone," I responded, and then I kissed her again as if that proved my point.

That night my dad made dinner and my mom went nuts over his green enchiladas. "Didn't I marry a saint, girls?" My mom laughed. She looked like she'd fallen in love with him all over again. Love was love, I concluded. It was what made people happy.

Cat turned to me and whispered, "Autumn, you're so lucky. Your parents are awesome."

"I know," I said, and wondered if something was wrong with her parents.

After dinner, Cat and I elected to walk Zeplin again. She confessed she adored animals even more than people. When we arrived at the park, I reached into my sweatshirt pocket and found half a joint. I noticed Cat watching me intently as I lit up. "Want some?" I asked.

"Okay, why not!" she said. "Will it make me feel less guilty?"

"Nothing to feel guilty about," I answered, even though I wasn't sure myself. She took a deep drag. After recovering from a coughing fit, she asked for another toke and broke out in a goofy smile.

"Cool," she said like an old time stoner.

Tiptoeing through the backdoor, we opened the fridge looking for munchies. Cat leaned on me in an adorable, crushed-out way. "Let's have a beer."

"Seriously? What's up with you tonight, girl?"

"I'm sick of being good. And I'm sick of being scared. I want to feel free and have fun."

I cracked two Coronas. We grabbed a bag of chips and went to my bedroom. Cat pounced on my bed.

"Hi," she giggled, wide-eyed. "I feel fan-tas-tic!"

"Me too, " I said, my own happiness elevated by hers. We lay on the bed, our eyes locked into each other's. I touched her arm. She ran her finger along my thigh, a match igniting a fire. I moved closer. So did she. The heat consumed us.

"No guilt?" I asked.

"Zero," she said, and kissed me on the lips. Our bodies had centuries of lust locked in their cells. Just as they knew what to do with a boy, they knew exactly what to do with another girl. Only for me, it was a thousand times more thrilling to be with Cat. Everything we did was electric. I loved her smooth, curvy, strong body and she seemed to love mine.

After that night we were inseparable. Cat slept over more than she went home. She loved my parents' laissez faire policy and they loved her friendly disposition. The first time my mother offered Cat a glass of Chianti Classico at dinner, her eyes bugged out, but she accepted, even poured herself a second glass. She seemed more and more game for exploring the wild side of life.

I thought it was odd that she still hadn't invited me to her house. After nearly a month, I couldn't help but ask, "When am I ever going to meet your family?"

"You'll be disappointed, Autumn. My parents are strict and full of rules. The only reason they let me stay over is because your dad is our dentist and they totally trust him. Anyway, I share a room with my little sister Missy, who's totally annoying. It's better here."

"Okay," I said, but it felt sad.

The following Friday evening, after Cat and I helped clean out our garage, my mom surprised me with the keys to her station wagon. We had mentioned that there was a bonfire at Stinson Beach and that we didn't have a ride.

"Have fun, you guys. You earned it," she said, and tossed me the keys. On the way down Sir Francis Drake Boulevard, we pulled over several times to make out and finally admitted we really just wanted to be alone. We decided to skip the party at Stinson and drove to Bolinas instead.

Finding a private cove, we sat on the white sand and watched the half-moon float like a canoe in the velvety sky. The waves spilled onto the shore as we talked about how magical it felt to have found each other.

"I'd like to tell just Mattie, since she's my oldest friend," I said. "It's getting strange hiding it from her. We tell each other everything." I was so in love I wanted everyone to know.

"No! We have to keep it a secret," Cat said. Her re-laxed expression turned grim. "You can't tell Mattie or anyone else. Promise me that!"

"I promise," I said, shocked by how alarmed she was.

"There's something you should know, Autumn. Our family is very religious. We go to church every Sunday. Nobody drinks or smokes or even swears in my house. We're Mormons. If my parents knew I've been drinking and getting stoned, or having sex with you, they'd flip out!"

I was in love with a Mormon girl? For all I knew, her father was a polygamist with three wives and that's why they had eight children. Personally, I considered myself an atheist, though I was still looking for signs. Cat was silent as we walked back to the car, as if her confession had drained all her energy. Despite our differences, I could feel our love was real and strong and would con-quer all obstacles.

It cooled off in mid-October. One Saturday morning, Cat and I were doing the laundry for my mom. We shook out the sheets and kissed each time we brought the cor-ners together.

"I think my mom might know," I told her.

"What? Well, don't admit it," Cat snapped.

"Not even to my mom? I know she'd be supportive. One of her best friends is a lesbian...and you know, more and more celebrities like Ellen are coming out all the time. It's practically considered normal to be gay."

"No! I told you. It's got to stay a secret. Stop being so pushy."

"Okay, sorry," I said, and she began to shake and cry.

"If my parents find out, they'll tell the bishop at our

church. And he'll try to rehabilitate me. If I can't be saved, they'll throw me out of the temple. I'll be excommunicated! I'll rot in hell for eternity and everyone will shun me. I had a gay cousin who got found out. He was an A student and a missionary and he still hung himself. Everyone loved him. Now, nobody talks about him anymore. It's like he never existed. Our family isn't like yours."

"Jeez, no wonder you're so scared," I said, as I held her and felt her tremble in my arms. "I had no idea it was so hard to be a Mormon."

Cat stepped away from me. "Don't joke," she said sternly. "I love my parents and I'd never want to hurt them! Our church says what we're doing is an abomination. We can never let anyone know, not your mother, not the coolest person on earth," she repeated. "Swear you'll never tell."

"I swear," I said. Then I whispered, "No one will ever know."

After that I made an effort not to touch her in public. I occasionally dropped the name of a phantom boy I had a crush on to my parents to divert their suspicions. I hated lying to them, but even more, I hated seeing Cat so frightened. I wanted her to feel safe and happy in our love. She wanted God to forgive her for loving me.

Over Thanksgiving break, we made love when my parents went out. We couldn't help ourselves. We'd kiss, then touch each other's breasts, or reach in between our legs and go absolutely crazy. Once we got started it was impossible to stop. Still, afterwards, Cat would cry. "I'm a sinner," she'd say, or, "This is so wrong."

"No, love is a good thing, Cat." I tried to convince her, but she felt ashamed and didn't want to talk about it.

During school hours, she insisted we avoid each other. Our soccer coach asked me if Cat and I were fighting and I said, "No. We're great." When she slept over now, she'd get into my twin bed with me for a minute, kiss me wildly, then jump out again and return to her own bed. She said she was afraid my parents would walk in. Periodically, she threatened not to stay over anymore and then a few days later, she'd show up at my door. She was tortured, split in two, whereas I was more on the side of love, regardless of the risks. I desperately wanted to help Cat feel at peace with being gay. I wanted her to continue loving me.

On a cold December afternoon, overcome with lust, I convinced her to meet me behind the bungalows after everyone had left campus. Hiding our love only fed my desire.

"We'll have a chance to talk things over. Strategize," I said. "We'll be completely safe."

"Okay," Cat said tentatively. I arrived first and spread my sweatshirt on the ground. I sat in a patch of bright sunlight. When Cat arrived she placed her sweatshirt beside mine and said, "Sorry I'm late."

"Everyone's gone," I said. "We're alone." She looked around and we both listened attentively for signs of life. It was perfectly still, deserted as it could be, the first time we'd been alone in days. I didn't want Cat to freak out, so I sat patiently waiting to see what she would say or do next. She looked around, then directly at me.

"You are so beautiful," I said. "I want you to be happy." She seemed to trust the moment and melted into my arms. Then she kissed me. No matter what else had become complicated and confusing, this part of our love was intact.

When I opened my eyes I saw a pair of clunky black pumps planted squarely in front of me.

"Girls," Miss Jasper, our principal, said, "Follow me to my office." And she briskly walked ahead of us.

"Oh God!" Cat bolted upright. "I'm dead."

"Don't worry," I said in an unconvincing voice. I was shaky myself. "We'll get out of this."

We moved in silence on Novocain legs to Jasper's office. Her shades were drawn and sweet air freshener masked the stale, musky odors. Miss Jasper paced the oak floor in her drab gray suit. Studying her pasty skin and beady eyes, I knew we were in big trouble. She looked like she'd never been in love or had sex with anyone.

Jasper scooted behind her desk and tapped a pencil on the tabletop with the syncopation of a metronome. Clearing her throat, she said, "Well, girls. This is a shock. Two such pretty, popular girls."

"We're sorry, Miss Jasper," Cat blurted. "We were just–"

"You've put me in an awkward position," she added. "Both A students, aren't you? On your way to excellent colleges?"

"Please, Miss Jasper," Cat pleaded. "We were just joking around. It was nothing."

I didn't know what to say that would make any sense or do us any good. Jasper rummaged through her desk drawer and pulled out forms that looked official. She thumbed through a few pages, studying the fine print. Then she looked up. "Now I have to decide how to proceed," she muttered.

Cat looked like a ghost.

"We didn't do anything wrong," I managed to say, and Jasper ignored me.

"I have to warn you that you are choosing a very rough road. Over the years, I have seen what happens to promising students who take these kinds of risks. Many wind up on drugs, lose their minds, and never recover. I can only imagine how difficult this will be for your parents–"

"Oh please, Miss Jasper. Don't tell them," Cat pleaded. "My parents are devout Mormons. They'll be devastated. It will kill my father. He has a weak heart. Our whole family will suffer. I'll do anything." She was breathless and petrified.

Jasper perched herself on the edge of her desk. Maroon lipstick was caked in the corners of her upturned mouth. She was relishing this! What a sick old bitch, I thought.

She resumed pacing, her heels clicking on the hardwood floor as though each step took her closer to a solution. "Both so talented...and beautiful, with such lovely figures." She paused at the window, opened the blinds and looked down onto the courtyard. I reached out to touch Cat's hand and she jerked it away. Jasper spun around, her eyes blazing, her cheeks flushed.

She picked up the forms and placed them back in her drawer. I took a deep breath and smiled at Cat, but her eyes were fully on Jasper. "I've decided to keep this just between us. On two conditions. Number one: each of you must come to my office once a week to discuss healthier ways to redirect your energies. Number two: You refrain from socializing with each other in order to curtail these urges. Agreed?"

"Agreed!" Cat said. "Thank you so much, Miss Jasper. You can count on us."

"Yeah," I said, confused but happy to get out of there. "Can we go now? I have to babysit."

"Yes, you may go, girls. Let's say next Wednesday at three o'clock sharp for you, Catherine, and the same time for you, Autumn, on Friday. We'll meet here in my office. And, of course, I don't want to hear about you two spending time alone together."

"That was scary. Thank God she decided not to tell," I said as we exited the schoolyard. I put my arm around Cat's shoulder and took a deep breath of fresh air.

"Don't touch me," she said, pulling away.

"Cat, she's just a lonely old pervert."

"Exactly. That's why we have to listen to her!"

My heart stopped. Jasper would keep the secret and destroy our love.

Cat and I walked home in unbearable silence. As we approached the intersection where we always parted reluctantly, I risked saying, "Cat, I love you."

"It's over, Autumn," she said. "I can't anymore." Her face was twisted and ugly. "Didn't you hear her? It's sick! You're sick!"

"No Cat. We can't listen to her," I cried, knowing she was already gone, destroyed by an avalanche of fear and shame.

"Shut up. Shut up. You're crazy. Your whole family is nuts. Just leave me alone," she screamed, and tore down the street without looking back. I watched her go. I watched the girl I loved run away from me. And there wasn't anything I could do to bring her back.

On The Bench

On her way home from the shelter, Dorothy stopped at Mel's Drugs for shaving cream, razors, cotton balls and Metamucil. She removed the creased list from her sweater pocket, lifted her reading glasses hanging from her neck and double-checked the needed items. She wanted to get it right this time so that Harry wouldn't scold her for forgetfulness. Today, he was off to play golf then promised to stop at the hardware store to pick up a new hose nozzle because the old one leaked. Dorothy insisted she could manage just fine without him at Mel's, and Harry conceded. All she had to do now was pay for the razors, shaving cream, cotton balls and Metamucil, and then she could go home with a sense of accomplishment. She was having lunch with someone. Oh yes, her sister Esther.

After folding filthy blankets in the community center's dark basement for hours, she was relieved to be shopping in an immaculate, well-lit place. Every Wednesday and

Friday morning, after the homeless had moved on to the Food Project's breakfast, Dorothy and other volunteers helped clean up the sleeping quarters. Dorothy was in charge of folding blankets and wiping down the benches. Others swept floors, picked up litter, and put things aside for the Lost and Found.

Dorothy was proud to be part of a community project that provided refuge for poor unfortunates–she liked doing good deeds for strangers–but at times the stench became unbearable. This morning, running a cloth over one of the benches, she touched a sticky substance that made her breakfast of oatmeal and raisins rise into her throat. Still, she was oddly drawn to these foul intensities, and returned each week to experience the beer, piss, and sexual smells that were absent in her own home.

Dorothy had been a schoolteacher, and since retiring three years before on Harry's advice, she donated her time to charity. She was good with people, friendly, smart and compassionate. If she wasn't helping out, the smallest things irritated her. Recently she found herself riled by Harry's habit of reading medical journals at the breakfast table. He never used to do that. Or did he? And, when he spoke harshly to Juanita, their devoted housekeeper of twenty years, Dorothy's blood boiled. She didn't speak up, only sighed or occasionally scowled. But when Harry left the room, Dorothy patted Juanita's hand. "Don't mind him," she said, and slipped her a twenty-dollar bill to compensate for the cruelty. Even though it was never right to treat people unkindly, Dorothy understood that as a cardiologist who dealt with life and death every day, Harry was under enormous pressure at the hospital. Sometimes at home, his top just blew off.

Still, it would have been comforting to have someone to talk to at mealtimes, someone with whom she could banter, watch PBS, and take evening strolls in the beautiful Berkeley hills where they lived. But Harry worked long hours and when he got home, he preferred to retreat to his study. Dorothy turned more and more to volunteer work for company, but sometimes she felt empty even when lending a hand.

The customer with dreadlocks and a ragged jean jacket ahead of her at Mel's checkout counter was a bum she'd never seen at the shelter or in the food lines. Dorothy had been volunteering at these same locations since retirement and was very familiar with the faces of the regulars. The name "Max" was embroidered with orange thread on the pocket of this stranger's jean jacket. Swinging tangled ropes of hair just inches from Dorothy's face, Max bobbed his head to rock and roll blasting from a portable radio in his hip pocket.

"Where's that money?" he said, searching his pockets. "I've been robbed–Oh. Oh. Here it is." He withdrew a Ziploc bag packed with crumpled bills and loose change. "I almost lost my cool. I'm fine now. Fine." Dorothy watched him and thought he panted just like her golden retriever. There was a wonderful exuberance in Max's smile. She understood his frustration, not being able to locate things even when they were close at hand.

For the past several months, she had been forgetting the names of things and people, which embarrassed her. Her closest friends said not to worry; it was happening to all of them as they aged, and they would laugh it off. But Dorothy didn't find her memory problem in the least bit funny.

The previous weekend, at the Mt. Zion Hospital's annual fundraiser, Dorothy was introduced to a young man who worked with Harry. Shaking his strong, warm hand, she asked how he liked working as a bagger at Safeway, and seeing the man's quizzical expression, she realized she'd made a terrible mistake. Later, Harry was livid. "He's a surgeon not a bagger, Dorothy."

"I got mixed up, Harry. He looks just like Alice's son."

"Alice's son has Asperger's!"

"Well, I didn't know that. For Pete's sake, Harry."

Harry was short with her when she missed her dental appointment because she had accidentally slipped into a matinee, and when he found her misplaced hairbrush in the refrigerator, he scolded her for not concentrating hard enough. But later, he looked sad and sorry when he stroked her cheek and said, "It's not your fault, Dorothy. Eventually, everyone's brain wears out, and for some it happens a little more quickly." Why did he constantly talk to her like a child? She had been a fine teacher, a voracious reader. She knew a thing or two.

Dorothy twisted a button on her cardigan, while concentrating on Max's purchases on the counter: a pack of disposable razors, the same brand she'd bought for Harry! Bugler tobacco, a bottle of Wite-Out and a Snickers bar. A good list to memorize. Everyone agreed games and puzzles were good medicine for the brain. She closed her eyes and repeated Max's list and when she opened her eyes again, she was pleased to see she hadn't forgotten anything!

While strolling the aisles earlier, Dorothy had wanted to buy Doritos, but refrained, trying to be good. Harry had her watching her cholesterol. He always had her watching something. Suddenly, she wanted to race back and get the Doritos, but was afraid she'd lose her place in line and be late for lunch.

"Eleven dollars forty-two cents," the checker said, and Max handed her wrinkled bills and his collection of coins.

"Don't spend it all in one place," he told the checker and winked at Dorothy. Well, he's certainly better off than the fellows at the center, she thought. And considerably more chipper.

On his radio, someone with a hoarse voice sang, "Tunnel of Love," and Max hummed along. Dorothy tapped her foot and continued to think about Doritos. She concentrated on the checker's nametag, "Loretta."

"There's a quarter. That's a penny. Nine dollars now. No? No. Only eight. Oh, you're right; you've got it now, girl." Max laughed wildly then pulled three pigeon feathers from his back pocket and fanned them out on the counter before the checker. "Here, dearest. An engagement present for you."

Then, suddenly, he turned to Dorothy and asked: "What do you think about Osama Bin Laden? Think he's dead? Well, he's not! Media hype. I saw him on Telegraph Avenue last night passing out The Street Sheet."

"Well, I had no idea," Dorothy said, setting her purchases on the counter. What an interesting homeless man Max was.

"Lots of people are alive that should be dead. Mistaken identities, deception, fraud." Max mumbled as he strolled out of the drugstore.

"What a weirdo," the checker said, ringing up Dorothy's items. "You have a good day now, Mrs. Richmond."

"You do the same, Lynette." Dorothy smiled, and walked outside.

Dorothy crossed the street to a French bakery, ordered a cheese Danish and a cappuccino, then sat on a wooden bench outside, surrounded by clay pots filled with cheerful impatiens and pansies. Harry would have a fit if he knew she was sneaking pastries again. The thought brought out a smile. "So there," she mumbled and stamped her foot. Lately, defying Harry was one of her greatest pleasures.

Max appeared with a Styrofoam cup of steamy black coffee and plopped down beside her. His grey pants were torn and disheveled; he had several missing teeth, and yet, he wore new Nike running shoes. Were they stolen or donated? People were so hard to figure out these days with all the hardships, scams, unemployment and foreclosures. Just when you thought you knew a person's circumstances, they shocked you with unforeseen, frequently devastating details.

"How's your mother?" Max asked matter-of-factly.

"She's dead, actually," Dorothy said in earnest, and was struck by the stink coming from Max: the familiar smell of the shelter and food lines, but also much like the steer manure she used in her garden. Harry refused to come near the garden because he hated to soil his trimmed fingernails. Instead he busied himself in his study researching everything that could go wrong with the heart.

"My mother's dead too," Max said. "It's a terrible shock to lose your mother, even when it's long overdue." Max lit the stub of a rolled cigarette yanked from his back pocket. Dorothy was about to tell Max where he could get a hot meal, but she couldn't remember the name of the Food Project or where it was located. Street names and phone numbers were going too.

"It's turned out to be a beautiful summer day," she said instead, and sipped her cappuccino. "You just never know with Berkeley summers."

"Summers aren't for sissies," Max answered cryptically, and removing a flask of whiskey from his backpack, poured a shot into his coffee cup. Then he rummaged around, brought out a spiral notebook, and flipped through pages of scrawl.

"Oh, are you a writer?" Dorothy bit into her Danish, experiencing a moment of exquisite pleasure. Why was Harry adamant about keeping her from such happiness?

"I speak seven languages, if that's what you mean. I record everything. Keeps my mind sharp." He pointed to his head and laughed freely. "I used to teach, mostly poetry but also history, mathematics, gold mining..."

Dorothy's heart skipped a beat. "Poetry. Really? In college I took some poetry courses. Would you care for some of my pastry? I really can't eat it all. It's quite yummy." Max shook his head and wrote something in his notebook.

"Not much of a bread eater myself. Clogs my lyrics."

Dorothy continued, "I even thought I had talent but my parents said it was a silly waste of time. Then I met Harry."

"Harry?"

"My husband. Dr. Harry Richmond. He's a cardiologist." Harry's name was still intact. "I'm Dorothy."

"Max."

"Yes, so I see." She studied his embroidered shirt pocket. "Max," she repeated over and over to herself. She didn't think she would ever forget his name.

Max poured another shot into his coffee. "Dorothy, my friend, let me buy you a drink." He attempted to pour whiskey into her cappuccino.

"No, Max. I really shouldn't. Not in the morning!" Dorothy giggled, crossed her legs, then kicked her feet out in front of her like a young girl on a swing. "Harry would have a heart attack!"

"Suit yourself." Max poured generously into his own cup. "You know, Dorothy, I'm fucking the CEO's daughter. She's crazy about it. A regular nympho." Max doubled over with laughter. Dorothy assumed he was drunk. Whiskey loosened the tongue. She'd seen it a thousand times at the shelter. Max needed help, decent food, a place to sleep, friends of his own kind. A person doesn't have to be drunk to feel crazy from loneliness.

"Max, do you take your meals at the Food Project?"

"No, not very often."

"I work there on Wednesdays and Fridays. The food is quite good, really. You ought to come. Today they're serving chocolate pudding."

"Maybe I will, Dorothy," he said and took another sip of his morning cocktail. "No harm in giving it a try! And are you sure you don't want a little nipper? Celebrate the moment!"

"Oh why not," she said. And Max poured her a shot. "Do you ever sleep at the shelter?" she asked.

"Sometimes I do. But usually it's full by the time I get ready for bed. I'm a night owl."

"Me, too!" Dorothy blurted excitedly.

"Besides, you can't trust those dirty rotten scoundrels." Max leaned in close to whisper to Dorothy. "I've had two Sony's plus my boots lifted. Merciless criminals. But I don't mind sleeping on the ground. I can hear my ancestors singing." He smiled broadly, revealing his ruined teeth.

"Harry thinks it's bad for my health to stay up late at night gazing at the moon. He's always trying to get me to drink warm milk and go to bed early. So bossy! 'Get your beauty rest, Dorothy,' he says, as if I were a little girl. I'd rather stay up listening to the creatures of the night." Dorothy closed her eyes and smiled dreamily. The liquor had warmed her body and awakened her spirit. "Everything's so alive when Harry's sleeping."

"Do you know if a train comes through here, Dorothy?"

"No, it doesn't, not here." She knew there was a BART station nearby, if that's what he meant, but she couldn't remember where it was.

Max kept drinking, taking straight shots; his coffee was long gone. Then he pulled out a newspaper and Wite-Out from his satchel. "I'm getting rid of Donald Trump. Every time I see his name on the page, I wipe it out." He removed Trump's name from the headlines, then relit his stub.

"That's very clever, Max. I guess that makes you an editor as well as a writer."

"You could say that, Dorothy." They both laughed. She hadn't had this much fun in years. "Come on girl, have another drink. Whiskey eases the soul into a hammock."

Dorothy hesitated then waved the drink away, still laughing. She bent over and pulled up her nylons. Looking down at her pumps, she remembered she was supposed to be home to have lunch with her sister, but at the moment she couldn't recall her sister's name. Then for an instant she couldn't remember her husband's name either. Panic set in. Her heart began racing. Her hands were clammy, and the impatiens and pansies in front of the bench became a smear of blinding color. Dorothy opened her pocket address book and flipped pages. Suddenly, there was Esther, her sister, at 510 843-0721. Yes. Dorothy took a breath. "Esther," she said aloud.

"Esther?" Max asked.

"My sister's name is Esther."

"Mine's Roberta."

"Who's Roberta?"

"My sis. You know, like Esther, Dorothy. But she's dead, like the rest of them. Sure you don't want another nip? Looks like you could use a little cheer."

"No. I really should be going. My husband will be worried. And I have a lunch date with my sister, Esther. I'm just a little concerned because I can't recall what time we were to meet. I think she's bringing her husband along today, or was that last time?"

"Steve Jobs is dead. Chalk it up to history," Max shouted, as if the death of this icon had just occurred.

"It's sad." She knew the name but couldn't recall if she genuinely felt sad about his passing.

"Worked for him for years. Tyranny is insidious. All is forgiven. Life is life. Death is death. We all keep changing places."

"I'm sorry you lost your job, Max."

"Didn't lose it, Dorothy. Quit. Dignity surpasses all weaknesses. " And he laughed heartily again. He certainly knew how to entertain himself. Dorothy was worried about Esther waiting, though by now she and Harry would be sipping their famous dry martinis on the patio and forgotten all about lunch.

Dorothy began to search for her car keys and her package slipped out of her hands. "Oh dear," she said as she leaned down to get it, and her eyeglasses, along with a pack of sugarless gum, fell out of her purse onto the ground. Max picked up the glasses and gum and the contents of the package and returned them all to Dorothy. "Take it easy, girl."

"Oh my! I am a little tired. Thank you so much, Max. You are a kind gentleman. I'm embarrassed to say I can't quite remember where I parked the car."

"And you are a lady of the highest echelon. Don't worry, my dear. I am a wizard at finding lost cars."

Max walked Dorothy to Mel's Drugs' parking lot. After checking several shiny black cars, Dorothy recognized the knitting on the front seat and Harry's medical journals on the back seat of their Lincoln sedan.

"Very sweet of you, Max. I don't know how I would have managed without you. Could I offer you something?" She pulled out her wallet.

"No, Dorothy. No need. But you could give me a lift to the food place. I must admit, that chocolate pudding is beginning to sound irresistible." He smiled, his darkened teeth exposed, and two rays of fine light coming through his eyes. "Feels like we've been buds forever, doesn't it Dorothy?"

"Yes, Max. It does. I'd love to drive you to the Food Project, but you'll have to be patient with me. I'll have to take it slow. At this time of day, I get a little tired, you know, and it's harder to remember things."

"Let me drive, Dorothy."

Dorothy hesitated. Would it be prudent to give up the car keys to a complete stranger? Max didn't feel like a stranger. Selfishly, it would be so restful to sit back and let Max drive. Of course, she'd insist that they wear their seat belts and keep the liquor in the trunk. And if they couldn't locate the Food Project, they could always take a drive, further north, past where road signs ended and only rolling hills, oak trees and cows marked the way. She couldn't remember the last time she'd seen a cow. She must have been a very young girl.

Dorothy looked up towards the hills where her handsome house was, where her husband and sister waited on the patio getting plastered on gin. Where each evening, after dinner, Harry sequestered himself in his study to research the mysteries of the human heart. Where everything was the same, but getting harder to remember and farther away.

The New Neighbors

Hello!

Here we are! We bought the fixer upper next door. And we brought you this bottle of wine to show you how happy we are to be your new neighbors and to apologize in advance for the racket. At first, we considered a teardown but decided there are enough salvageable features to maintain the original charm, so we're only remodeling. Still, it should significantly jack up your property value as well as ours. I know. It's time to say goodbye to linoleum floors and aluminum windows. Exactly how long did that older woman live here without touching a single thing?

You must drop by for tea or coffee and see the place before the facelift. And please use our driveway to turn your cars around. Not at all. And when the job's done we'll celebrate the new girl's looks with a champagne toast. How about a hug? Oh, these are our dogs. Smarty and Marty. They bark but they're friendly like we are. Go ahead. Pet them. Oh. Look. They're wagging their tails! How cute is that?

Oh hi! You startled me. I was just getting the paper. Sorry we haven't been in touch. It's been pure madness. One disaster after the other! While ripping out the wall-to-wall orange shag rug, circa the middle-ages, we discovered nothing but rotted plywood underneath. We had to bite the bullet and lay down a new subfloor in addition to the oak floor. I'm not even going to mention the price per foot. And trust me, gutting the kitchen wasn't cheap either. What a mess. We went for a rustic Italian look with imported Tuscan tiles and wormwood cabinets. If you're going to do it, do it right. Am I right? All Hans-grohe fixtures in the bathrooms, of course. Tasteful but not gauche. We can't even look at the receipts. But hopefully it will all be worth it in the end. Fingers crossed.

Just a heads-up, we're tearing out the driveway and the decks. Sorry in advance for the jackhammers. Workers coming and going all day long, one can hardly think. I know. It's challenging. Well you can imagine what it's been like for us not having a kitchen for three months. Total and utter chaos. But wait till we see the results, right? Fingers crossed.

We're done! It's done. I'm still in shock. We insist you come by tonight and take a peek. We'll crack open the bubbly as promised. Dom Perignon. Only the best for our very understanding and tolerant sweet neighbors. Pop! I know. Isn't it gorgeous? Well, we tried. Thanks. Have another glass. Have a cracker. You're the best.

What happened? How did your tree fall into our yard? What do you mean, "things happen?" What kind of fucking excuse is that? The tree expert said what? The integrity of the roots was compromised by a disproportionately elongated limb. What kind of mumbo jumbo is that? Marin Arborist? Who the hell is he? You could have consulted with us before you just cut the whole thing down. Now we'll lose half our shade. FYI we wrapped our entire concept for this remodel around a Mediterranean shade garden. Frankly, everything has happened so fast, my head is spinning. I can't understand a word you're saying. Frankly, I could use a Xanax. We were up all night wondering if you'd cut the tree down on purpose. Why would you do that? We have no fucking idea.

If we'd known you were going to impulsively chop down trees, and destroy our landscape, we never would have bought the damn house. You are scenery thieves. Suddenly our living room window is exposed to the road, the full circus of humanity strolling by. Who knows if we're even safe here anymore with everyone looking in? Do you have any idea how much a high-end remodel costs? You've totally fucked up our investment.

Stay away from our dogs. You make them nervous. And excuse us if we don't have time for a cocktail. Or tea and cookies. We're selling the house and moving to LA where we can flip houses like pancakes. We leave you to oversee your unstable arboretum.

Thursday: Brokers' open. Sunday: Buyers' open. Little triangular sandwiches, finger food. Perrier. We should get top dollar. The market's exploding. You've already witnessed the beauty we carved out of a shithole, so it shouldn't be a surprise. Don't bother to say thank you. Offers are rolling in despite the blighted landscape. Pending. Sold. Inspections. Last minute touch-up paint and fence repairs. Packing. Up and down stairs. Boxes boxes boxes. Here we go. The movers' truck loaded like a gun. Bang! So long suckers! Bye-bye country living. Oh look! Here come your new neighbors with a bottle of wine.

Lucky Boy

In our tiny town of Moss, there is a tradition that an up and coming man should marry his first wife before he turns thirty, divorce her before he turns fifty, and then marry his second, much younger and enviable wife, preferably in her twenties but no older than thirty-five, after he has made his fortune. In his first marriage, he is expected to have two to three children, and in his second, only one golden child, known as Lucky Boy, even if the child turns out to be a girl.

After he divorces his first wife, and before his marriage to his second wife, he is expected to send alimony to his angry first wife, and to lavish his sad children with gifts to compensate for his absence.

For a period of at least six months but no more than five years, he is expected to date a variety of Moss socialites, but never more than three times in succession so that he will garner a reputation as the most eligible bachelor in Moss. His abandoned children are expected to hate their mother for letting their father go, and to adore their father for his wild and preposterous life.

Once the father has married his second wife everything is expected to change. The man will impregnate his new wife with the golden child, and his generosity towards his children will come to a screeching halt when he claims a grave financial downturn. The children of his first wife are expected to feel gypped, and his first wife, forced to work in the Whole Foods deli for $12 per hour, to feel homicidal.

The perceived health of the father's new love relationship will absolve him of guilt, and he will easily convince himself that his failed marriage was entirely his first wife's fault.

Meanwhile, his golden child, Lucky Boy, will become aware of his privilege and wealth. He will feel a mixture of gratitude and guilt when his father takes him on European bike tours during prep school holidays. When he receives a Ferrari on his sixteenth birthday, he will shun his half brothers and sisters to avoid their nasty stares.

In this particular story, Lucky Boy is Muffin Brookfield and she has recently married Garth Phipps III, a lucky boy himself. In Moss, the tradition for lucky boys who marry other lucky boys has a slightly different trajectory. Unlike the self-made man who begins by marrying someone beneath him, Garth is expected to marry his equal, someone born at least as beautiful and rich as himself. He will not be expected to leave her for a second younger wife though he will be expected to have many short-lived affairs, the bulk of which will take place with shy girls who speak a foreign language, which is his version of being discreet. It is also within tradition for

Muffin to marry someone even richer and more comely than herself and to never entertain the notion of leaving her husband, even if there is evidence that he is guilty of white-collar crime.

Both Garth and Muffin have followed tradition impeccably, and are considered to be an ideal Moss couple. At the moment, Muffin is a fresh, spunky twenty-six and Garth is a mature twenty-seven who looks thirty because of his sense of purpose and fitted Italian suits. Once high school Homecoming king and queen, they attended Harvard, each graduating at the top of their class. Garth went on to Yale law school, then joined his father-in-law's international law practice. Muffin became a fearless fundraiser, hosting World Hunger luncheons on her sprawling lawn.

Muffin's smile is as permanent as a snapshot; her immaculate clothing appears to be just removed from the dry cleaners' protective cellophane. Her blonde hair pulled tightly into a Sharon Stone knot at the back her head makes her look alternately younger and older than she really is.

There she is now, strolling down the walkway from her brick house toward the tennis court with a glass in one hand and an ice bucket in the other. Let's follow her and see what we can learn about her Lucky Boy Life.

Each afternoon this summer, at four o'clock, you will find her here. After saying goodbye to the girls from the club, she lets her hair down and dons a visor to protect her porcelain white skin from the punishing rays of the sun.

Before her husband returns from his law office, she perches on the shaded bench under the maple tree and drinks her gin neat until she is just shy of plastered. Being slightly blotto at dusk is a strong tradition in Moss, passed down from mother to daughter as well as from father to son. Muffin knows that her drinking days are numbered. Pregnancy will soon require bubbly water replace gin. But for now, a pleasant afternoon buzz is a perfectly acceptable way to pass the time in Moss. It is after all tradition, and Muffin is a girl who happens to be a Lucky Boy.

The breeze that picks up is refreshing. Muffin loves the way it swirls her hair around and cools her alcohol-heated face. When a branch from the maple tree suddenly breaks off and plunges into the ice bucket beside her, just missing her head, Lucky Boy is reminded once again of her good fortune, privilege and divine destiny.

And then, the whole tree comes down on top of her.

Uncle Sammy

It's a warm and lazy Los Angeles afternoon in 1961. I'm twelve going on thirteen, and savoring the last easy-going days of summer vacation from junior high, a time when I believe that a Coppertone tan is my ticket to a popular boyfriend, that I will soon graduate from an AA to a C cup simply by doing push-ups in gym class, and that my family is the safest place to be on earth. My father, Benjamin Zimmerman, an accountant, says that ever since Kennedy clobbered Nixon, even the French envy us our movie star president, our Zenith color TVs and two-car garages. My mother, Esther Zimmerman, says my father is the most reliable man alive and we owe him for everything we have. Joanie, my nine-year-old sister, says almost nothing and follows me everywhere. Currently, she's dog-paddling with her girlfriends at Rancho pool, leaving me to concentrate on Catcher in the Rye, a novel about a kid named Holden Caulfield who thinks everything is bullshit.

Leaning against the brick wishing well my dad built singlehandedly in June, I look up from my book to the front porch where my mother and Uncle Sammy are standing close together, with the breeze blowing through their hair, smoking cigarettes. My mother only smokes a couple of times a year, so I know this is an important cigarette. Her auburn streaks shine in the sunlight and her perfect teeth glisten when she smiles. My father's youngest brother, Sammy, dressed in his bright white starched uniform, looks more like a sailor than a milkman. His hair is so dark it has a blue sheen. He's tall and slim and my mother says he looks like Errol Flynn. Even though he's only a milkman, he's the closest our family has to a movie star, especially if you compare him to the rest of the Zimmerman brothers, stumpy, half bald businessmen. He's the wild card in an everyday deck of cards. Like Holden Caulfield, he says and does whatever is on his mind, which includes offering us bursts of magic that make life appear more amazing than it really is.

For instance, today when he dropped by on a break from his Adohr milk route, he cha-cha-ed across the lawn juggling two glass bottles of milk in the air. Then he spun himself like a top and managed to catch both bottles before they smashed to the ground. Mom and I watched with our mouths open. He took a bow and we applauded. But now my mother is getting riled up as they talk on the porch. Because of some trouble he got into not long ago involving gambling and drinking, my father doesn't like him to come over when he's not home. "Too unpredictable" my father says, "Not a good influence on the kids." My mother usually defends my uncle. "He's reformed, Ben." She's right. Uncle Sammy is trying hard to be good. He stopped gambling and is selling milk now instead of whiskey.

The conversation heats up on the porch and soon their heads start bobbing up and down and side-to-side. It looks like they're fighting. It doesn't take too much strain on my part to overhear my mother say, "Sam, Ben will be here any minute. You know how he gets."

Don't misunderstand. My father loves his brother. He's the first one to loan him money to get out of a jam, and he's the only brother Uncle Sammy comes to for advice. But my father has the idea that he needs to be around to prevent bad things from happening to us.

My uncle stamps out his cigarette on the banister and walks away from my mother, looking dejected. Shaking out his lanky body, he looks directly at me and lights up a smile, then cha-chas down the front steps. My mother stays on the porch, leaning against the railing. She takes a slow drag on her cigarette, and blows smoke up into the cloudless blue sky. With her hands she smooths out the creases in her yellow sundress. Sometimes, watching how she acts around him, I wonder if she wishes she'd married Uncle Sammy instead of my father.

During the war, Sammy taught women to dance at a hotel in the Catskill Mountains where my mother spent her summer vacations. The story goes that they dated for a while, but when my father returned from fighting Nazi's and drove up to the hotel to visit his brother, my mother and father fell in love. I think the reason my dad is so good to my uncle is because he feels guilty about stealing my mother away.

"How is my Adohr-able niece?" Sam sings out while performing fancy dance steps on the grass. He's turned his charm on me now, and though he's putting on a good show, there's a cloud of disappointment in his eyes. At moments like this one, I feel sorry for him because even though he's handsome and talented, he seems lonely because he can't get a girlfriend of his own. "Nothing sticks," my father says and leaves it at that.

"What a doll," Uncle Sammy says, hugging me a little too hard. "Goddamn it! Look at those big brown eyes! Hell, exactly like your mother's." It's true. Everyone says I look just like her when she was my age. Besides gambling and drinking, my uncle swears even more than Holden Caulfield, who's famous for swearing and not even a real person. "It won't be long before you'll have to fight the boys off. Maybe you do already. Hell, you could hypnotize anybody with those gorgeous eyes." He turns to look at my mother then back at me.

Without warning, he swoops me up in his arms and glides me around the bright green manicured lawn my dad mows every Sunday morning. Uncle Sammy spins me out, snaps his fingers over his head like a Flamenco dancer, then reels me back in. His body is like a radiator. If you stand too close, you could get burned. He glances at my mother every time he pivots. He spins me faster, holds me too tight, as he dances me to the edge of our driveway.

I spot Mr. Alder watching us from across the street while he waters his roses. It feels creepy to be dancing with my uncle in front of the neighbors. I'm relieved when Uncle Sammy finally lets me go. I can breathe again. I step back from his long shadow, as he reaches into his pocket and hands me a dollar bill.

"What's this for? I didn't do anything," I say, taking the dollar anyway.

"Oh yes. You're the dancer. I only provide the wind." Then he hugs me against his uniform, and besides the smell of sweat, there's a hint of alcohol on his breath.

"So, what's my little genius reading these days?" he says, and pulls out a handkerchief to wipe his forehead.

"I'm not a genius," I say. "Just call me Lorrie. *Catcher in the Rye.*"

"Sounds good!"

My mother crushes out her cigarette and comes down from the porch. "Off to work, Sam?" she says.

"You guessed it, Esther. No time to waste."

Just before he takes off in his Adohr truck, he shouts, "Hey Lorrie, catch!" and he tosses me a quart of my favorite chocolate chip ice cream. Then he speeds away down Veteran Avenue.

One night a few months later, Uncle Sammy calls to say he's got some terrific news he wants to deliver in person.

It's my father who answers the phone and says, "Okay, Sam. Then come for dinner tonight."

We're all sitting around the kitchen table, eating my mother's meatloaf with mashed potatoes, waiting anxiously to hear the news. Uncle Sammy is bouncing his leg, and grinning, and hardly eating a thing.

"Don't keep us in suspense, Sam," my father says.

"Yeah, Sam," my mother adds. "Don't be a tease."

"Well, kiddos, I finally met the girl of my dreams!" He looks at each of us to see our reaction, then proceeds to rattle off the story of how he met Cinda, who both my father and mother will later refer to as the "shiksa" or the "bimbo," but not in front of Uncle Sammy. With him, they pretend to be happy as he shares how they met. "I was at a casino in Gardena, but not gambling, Ben, so don't worry. Just went to meet some dames," he says, slapping my father's arm. Apparently, Cinda was the most gorgeous cocktail waitress he'd ever seen. "We hit it off right away. She laughed at every goddamned joke I told! Then after her shift we talked into the night. Long story short, she convinced me to quit Adohr and go to work as a card dealer at her casino. She hooked me up with the boss the very next day! So, gang, I'm moving to Gardena and I start work on Monday. I'll be making three times what I make at Adohr, enough to provide for my future wife and buy her a house!"

"Wife? So fast? You hardly know her yet, Sam."

"It's the real thing, Ben. I'm not going to let this one get away," he says, looking over at my mother who gets up to clear the dishes, knocking over her water glass.

Sammy and Cinda elope to Las Vegas but they invite their friends and family to the reception, which takes place at a social hall in Gardena. It's early November and there's a chill in the air as I walk with my mother, father and Joanie from the parking lot into the beige stucco building that looks like my high school gymnasium. It's almost as cold inside as outside, and the air smells like perfume, whiskey and bug spray. Uncle Sammy's Gardena friends are milling around, gulping bourbon drinks and flicking cigarettes into glass ashtrays the size of serving platters.

"They're half crocked already," my father mutters to my mother, then takes off to join his brother Irv at a corner table where they will discuss business investments like they always do at weddings and bar mitzvahs.

Cinda comes rushing up to us, "Finally!" she squeals, waving a champagne glass in the air. She looks cheesier than I imagined. Her face is caked in thick makeup and her glittery pink dress is as tight as Saran Wrap. Latching onto my mother's arm, she jabbers away like they're old friends even though they just met. Mom listens politely, but I can tell by her frozen smile that she hates Cinda as much as I do.

While Cinda greets other guests, I overhear Mom whisper to my Aunt Rachel, "He could have had anyone."

"Not the one he wanted," Aunt Rachel answers.

"I'm thirsty," I say and join my older cousin, Shelly, a rebel, at the bar where she is spiking her Shirley Temple with people's leftover champagne.

"What a bullshit wedding," she says, and I agree so that she'll think I'm as cool as she is at sixteen. "I'm going outside for a cigarette. Wanna come?"

"No, not now," I tell her afraid she'll make me take a puff.

When Uncle Sammy spots me standing alone at the bar, he grabs Cinda by the hand and struts across the room. His silky black hair is slicked back with pomade and his eyes sparkle like dark jewels. Today he really does look like a movie star.

"Lorrie, honey," he bellows. "This is the crazy girl I bribed into marrying me."

I almost say we already met, but Cinda shrieks, "Oh Sammy, stop!" and makes goo-goo eyes at him. Holden Caulfield would go nuts describing her phony personality. I ask for a sip of her champagne, which she gives to me, giggling like someone with a screw loose. "She's so cute, Sammy!"

But he's gone already, on the dance floor with Aunt Sylvia who weighs three hundred plus. Holding her close, he dips her like she's a sexy young girl, then whispers in her ear.

"Oh Sam," I hear her howl with laughter. "You're terrible." Which I know means he just told her a dirty joke.

"I'm going to visit the little girl's room, Sugar," Cinda says.

When Uncle Sammy finishes his show-off dance with Aunt Sylvia, he strolls out to where my mother is standing alone on the patio looking up at the stars. I guess he asks her to dance because she follows him back inside. He holds her close and she shuts her eyes as they glide across the dance floor like smooth professionals.

When Cinda returns from the ladies' room, she stands beside me like I'm her date. Her glossy pink lips quiver as she watches her new husband twirl my mother in circles. "They dance good together, huh?" she says to me, then trips on her high heel and just barely catches herself by grabbing onto a folding chair.

I see Uncle Irv poke my father who then stands up. With his arms crossed in front of his chest, he watches Mom and Uncle Sammy's fancy moves. When my mom and uncle catch sight of him, they move apart and wave.

After Sammy moves to Gardena, an hour away by car, we hardly see him, but he calls my father to report his latest business successes. Apparently, he and Cinda are both managers at the casino now, and soon will be putting a down payment on a house, buying a boat, maybe digging a swimming pool.

"One *fercocktah* story after the other," my father grumbles when he tells us the latest. I know my mother is upset with my father's lack of faith in his brother. She wants us all to believe things are getting better so that she can.

"Let's just wait and see, Ben," she says.

When he stops calling altogether, my mother tries to get in touch. She calls his house and no one answers. None of the relatives have heard from him either. Eventually an operator says that his line has been disconnected. Mom thinks about calling him at work, then realizes she doesn't even know the name of the club where he works. My parents are about to drive down to Gardena to find out what's happened to him when he shows up at our door in a maroon velvet outfit my mom calls a lounging suit. He's sweaty and out of breath, and looks more like he's been wrestling than lounging.

"A complete and utter goddamn mix-up," he says, coming inside and kissing each of us on the cheek. "I knew you'd be worried, so I drove right the hell over here." Apparently, the phone company lost his check and turned off his service by mistake. "I straightened out the whole damn mess and everything is A-OK now." After a few jittery minutes, he worms his way toward the front door, his exit ticking in the air like an alarm clock. On his way out, he gets all emotional, promising to bring Cinda next time. "She misses the hell out of you guys," he says. "We both love you to death. Sorry to run off but I've got a mega-managers meeting." Whatever that is.

As soon as he's gone, my father says, "When am I going to get a little peace in my own house?" and goes into the den to watch *Father Knows Best.* We follow like dazed sheep.

Two months later, my father comes home early from work looking gloomy. He takes off his glasses and rubs his eyes. We gather around him to find out what's wrong.

"I knew it," he says, sighing heavily, then plops down onto the couch. "Sam caught Cinda fooling around with the blackjack dealer from the club, an Italian kid half her age. Sam threw the both of them out on their tails, and that's all she wrote." Then looking down at his hands, he adds, "I invited him to dinner Sunday, Esther. We're all he's got now."

My mother spends all day Sunday cooking and cleaning. Joanie and I set the table and pick carnations from the yard. "We'll make it festive to cheer him up," Mom says, smiling. We wait more than an hour before we sit down at the table and eat without him. Nobody talks except to say pass this and pass that. But there's a lot of loud chewing and clanging of silverware.

Then while we're watching Ed Sullivan, there's a knock at the door. My dad says, "Lorrie, see if it's him."

"Hi kid," Sam says when I open the door. He's wearing dark sunglasses, like a gangster. He doesn't smile or try to hug me. In fact, he walks right past me in his black shirt, white silk tie, and suede shoes. He heads straight for the den, running his hands over the thick paint of the Laguna seascapes in the hall, touching each wave with his fingertips like he's reading braille.

"Sorry I'm late, kiddos. It's been a hell of a complicated day." His hands are as fidgety as his feet. He lights a cigarette with a snappy silver lighter and takes a couple of puffs. He's bony, pale and doesn't resemble a movie star anymore, well maybe a movie star with cancer.

My mother turns down the volume on the TV and says, "I've got plenty of leftover pot roast, Sam. Let me heat it up for you." Standing beside him, she rests her hand on his wrist as if her touch will hypnotize him into eating something. "Are you all right, Sam?" she asks. He turns away from her, and walks over to the mantel where the family photographs are lined up. When he gets to Mom and Dad's wedding picture, he blows giant smoke rings at their young smiling faces.

"Ben," he says to my dad, "could I talk to you for a minute, privately?"

"Okay, Sam. Let's go out on the patio." My father, who's wearing his Hawaiian shorts and a white T-shirt, marches ahead of him like a Boy Scout leader.

Joanie cuddles up closer to Mom on the couch and together they concentrate on a boring act with elephants walking on planks. I sneak away, grab an empty water glass from the kitchen and press it against the back door, straining to hear my father and uncle's conversation.

"Sam, I'm sorry, I just can't keep sticking my neck out," I hear my father say. "I've got a family to support. Maybe the gambling business isn't for you. Now that Cinda's out of the picture, maybe you'd like to get something a little more reliable?"

"I understand completely, Ben. Sure. I know what you're saying. I've been thinking the same thing myself. I'm going to do it, absolutely, save my neck. Start fresh."

"Maybe you'd like to go back to Adohr. I bet they'd be thrilled to have you."

"That's a brilliant idea. Why didn't I think of it? Why couldn't I come up with one perfect goddamned idea?"

"Sam, don't get yourself all excited."

"My big brother always knows exactly what he wants and goes after it! Why can't I do that? God damn it to hell, can you answer me that?"

"Sam, I didn't mean to upset you..."

"I know, Ben. No one's to blame but myself. I've fucked everything up, ruined my whole goddamned life."

Is he crying? I press the glass harder against the door. I want to hear everything, know everything, so I can understand who my uncle really is. After a long silence, I crack the door slightly, and witness an amazing thing: Uncle Sammy is bent over with his head hanging down, and he's sobbing like a baby. His whole body shakes while he cries. My father grabs his taller younger brother by the shoulders and straightens him up.

"Look at me, Sam," he says. "For God's sake, show some self-respect." Sam squints and sniffles and blows his nose with a handkerchief while my dad fishes in his pockets.

Only when Dad piles a bunch of bills in Uncle Sammy's palm, does his body start to relax. He looks at my father with a helpless, goofy grin.

"Remember, Sam, this is the last time I can do this," Dad says, trying to sound tough but I can tell he's just sad.

"You're a jewel, Benny. Thank you. I'm going to get back on track, no more bullshit."

"Lorrie, where are you?" my mother yells. "Get back in here and leave the men alone."

"What's wrong?" Joanie asks me.

"Uncle Sammy is crying. "Then I ask my mother if he's having a nervous breakdown and my sister chimes in.

"Is he Mom? Is he going bananas?" Mom says we shouldn't think that way. She pats the cushion beside her and I sit down. Then she puts an arm around each of us.

"Uncle Sammy is having a rough time because of the break up with Cinda, but things will pick up soon. They always do," she says. But her eyes are full of tears.

For the next year, I'm preoccupied with Johnny, my first real boyfriend, who kisses like he really means it, and leaves love notes in my locker. Everyone at school likes him, and when I invite him to our house for dinner, my parents seem impressed too. What they don't know is that sometimes on the weekends, we sneak a couple of Johnny's father's beers, and I let him feel me up. But that's our secret. It makes our love stronger and more thrilling.

A nutcase has struck down our country's handsome hero, and on the first New Year's Eve after Kennedy's assassination, my parents go out with Aunt Rachel and Uncle Irv to forget about how devastated they all are. I'm in charge of babysitting Joanie, who is so annoyed at being babysat at eleven that I decide to cheer her up by getting her drunk. A jigger of Smirnoff's goes into each of two tall glasses of Sunkist orange juice. Handing Joanie her first screwdriver, I clink glasses and say, "Happy New Year."

Soon we are buzzed, and get into my mother's warehouse of Revlon makeup. Joanie rummages through the closet and over her pajamas throws my mother's fur coat. Acting sophisticated, she steps into a pair of her backless heels. She struts around the living room like a contestant while I play the MC for the Miss America ceremonies. We giggle hysterically until we're exhausted.

Then we curl up on the sofa to watch "Creature Features." Frankenstein chases a pale, frightened girl through a castle while we devour hot buttered popcorn. I'm determined to stay up until the ball drops, but poor Joanie conks out after fifteen minutes.

At 10:30 there's a knock at the front door and I wonder if Johnny snuck out of his parent's party to come see me. Through the screen door, I see Uncle Sammy looking like someone's been chasing him. There are beads of sweat suspended on his forehead. He flashes me an embarrassed grin and I think, "Now what?"

He hasn't shaved, his clothes are a wrinkled mess and there are dark circles under his eyes. He seems to be getting older faster than anyone else in my family.

"Hi ya doll," he says when I unlatch the screen door. "You look great. Is your Dad here? Boy oh boy, it's freezing out tonight." He rubs his palms together and let's out a sigh. I can smell the booze from six feet away.

"Geez, look at you," he says, staggering into the hallway. "Wearing lipstick and all. So grown up already." When he looks deeply into my eyes, I look away.

He is trying to act sober but there's no doubt he's plastered. He braces himself at the bar and helps himself to straight bourbon, swallowing it with a handful of pills. I stare at him like a witness observing from the other side of a two-way mirror, trying to identify who he is now compared to who I remember he once was.

"I'm in a bit of a pickle, doll," he confesses, sweat dripping down his temples. "Jesus, you're goddamn gorgeous. Anyway, kid, my car payment is due and the dealer is being a real asshole. Says he's going to break both my arms, imagine, if I don't pay up tonight. Tonight!" He laughs and the sound strangles in his throat. "I hate to ask, sweetheart, but would you happen to have a few dollars you could loan your old uncle for just a couple of days? Pay you back with interest! Promise."

I'm no idiot. By now, I know my uncle is 100 per cent bullshit. He's lying about the car dealer, about everything, but I can't just throw him out. I imagine my father listening to this same crap, and giving him the money anyway. So when he scolds me for doing such a stupid thing, I'll look him straight in the eye and say, "Dad, I did it because you would have." Like my father, I'm hoping that giving Sam the money will keep him from getting hurt or doing something crazy. I swallow the knot that's swelling in my throat.

"I've got some babysitting money and my dad keeps cash in his underwear drawer," I answer. "I'll be right back."

He lights up a Camel. "Want one?" he says, offering the pack.

"I don't smoke," I say.

"Crazy. I keep forgetting you're only sixteen."

"I'm fourteen," I correct him.

In my bedroom I dump the money I've saved into a paper bag, and in my parent's bedroom, open the top drawer of my dad's dresser where he hides his cash. I begin counting, piling the money on their bed. I'm up to $97.50 when I feel Uncle Sammy behind me. He's too close. Too something. My heart speeds up like I've entered a marathon. I have to keep moving. I pull my mother's collection of purses off the closet shelf and dump them on the bed.

"God, you're a knockout," he says. "Doesn't everyone tell you you've got your mother's sexy eyes exactly?"

Pretending not to hear his creepy words, I frantically rummage through Mom's purses, looking for loose change.

Suddenly, he plunks down beside me and rests his large, hot hand on mine. "Is this everything, Esther?"

Now he thinks I am my mother. His breath smells sour and his hand is on fire. When he snakes his arm around my back, I freeze. My world shrinks to a small dark corner of my mother's purse where pennies and bobby pins lie buried in lint. It's impossible to locate the compass I need to guide me out of this mess.

Sammy takes a deep drag on his cigarette and blows a cloud of smoke into my hair, then begins to stroke the tight muscles at the base of my neck. "Oh, you're so tense, honey. We've got to get these knots to relax," he says, kneading my shoulders like dough he wants to shape into something that belongs to him.

Out of the corner of my eye, I see him wave his cigarette in the air, and drops ashes on the carpet. Reeking of alcohol, he leans more heavily on my shoulder, whispering in my ear, "How about a kiss, sweetheart? Just for old time sake."

I turn to face him. He's unzipped his pants, and his thing is in his hands.

"Wanna touch it?"

There it is, staring at me through the opening in his grey slacks. A fat worm with a mushroom cap, jutting out into the room, as otherworldly as an alien's telescope. This is the worst moment of my life. My body feels like it's sinking into quicksand and my ears are hot and buzzing, as the room tilts at a strange angle, all my senses off kilter. Even my uncle's raspy voice seems farther and farther away.

"So you thought your mother had her cherry when she married your father," he slurs. Staring at my uncle's stiff penis, an event I'm certain will ruin my sex life, which hasn't even begun yet, I want to call out to Joanie, but my voice stops working.

He pushes me flat on my back and falls on top of me, eyes shut like he's trying to turn me into nobody at all. With his big sweaty hands, he holds my skinny girl arms down on the bed. Then he tries to pull down my pajama bottoms but I squeeze my legs together. He swears under his breath and yanks harder at the elastic band of my pj's. I can't let this happen, I tell myself, although I'm afraid I'm losing the battle. The cottage cheese ceiling is closing in and I can hardly breathe.

Pinned like a butterfly to my parents' king-size bed, staring up at my uncle's damp strands of hair hanging inches from my face, I understand that whatever happened or didn't happen between him and my mother years ago, their twisted love story is threatening to destroy me now.

My anger lights a match in the dark, and a powerful flame shoots up to reveal a way out. I am not my mother. This is not my destiny! Not my life. The first thing that ignites is my voice.

"Lorrie!" I shout my name like a benediction. "I'm Lorrie!" Uncle Sammy lifts his head and opens his bloodshot eyes. He glares at me, eyes bulging out of his head like his brain is working double time to figure out where he is, and what the hell he's doing. Then he keels over on the bed like someone has shot him in the back. He drops so dramatically it seems fatal. He doesn't move. Doesn't say a goddamn word. I nudge him with one finger. Nothing. I stare at him. Is he dead? How am I going to deal with a six-foot corpse, especially my drunken uncle's corpse? I start to panic. My head pounds like a heart. I feel like a murderer who has to get rid of the evidence. Then he takes a big noisy drunken breath. He's alive. His body twitches and he's snoring loudly but he's definitely out cold, as good as dead. Now, how to get him out of the house before my parents come home, before my father finds him here and kills him and goes to jail for life. I need Joanie's help.

I'll tell her everything. And together we'll splash cold water on his face like they do in gangster films. And when he comes around, we'll scream in unison, "Zip up your pants, and get the hell out of our house, you bastard." We'll scare the hell out of him. Forgetting the money on the bed, he'll stagger out the front door, slip inside his ratty old Chevy and screech away from the curb. Maybe he'll get killed in a car crash. Joanie and I will make a secret pact not to tell anybody he was here on New Year's Eve and tried to steal more than money from our family.

I leave him there, curled up like a caterpillar, and race into the den to get Joanie. Sitting on the couch beside my little sister, I gently wake her from a dream by whispering her name. "Joanie. Joanie."

Face Work

My fifty-one-year-old, brainiac wife Ann prided herself on being the only woman in her book group who hadn't had any work done. Her friend Marlene had been cut several times, first the eyes, then the remainder of her face, and on her last birthday her husband treated her to cheek implants. Currently she was entertaining the idea of elevated boobs. Ann thought it was totally disgusting. "So artificial and anti-feminist," she ranted. "Why can't anybody just age naturally anymore?"

"Honey, sometimes people feel better when they get a little lift and then they're nicer to everyone else," I responded.

"Are you implying I'm not nice?" she shouted, stomping her bare feet on the floor. Ann has a quick temper so I try not to incite her.

"No, sweetheart, you're great. I'm just saying some people..." And we left it at that.

I'm a car salesman at a Jaguar dealership and I work with a lot of thirty-year-old whiz kids. Overnight, I'd become the old guy on the lot. One single guy stands out. Jake is thirty-one and perpetually upbeat. Since the first of the year, he'd sold twice as many cars as I had even though he's a rookie and I've been with the company for twenty-five years. He was killing it, I believed, because he's fucking beautiful. I mean, gorgeous ink black hair, greased and swept back like a young Robert DeNiro, deep-set dark eyes, snow white teeth and a phony air-brushed Caribbean complexion. Women love buying cars from him. While he explains the car's special features, they feel like they're engaged in foreplay, and right after they sign they will have full on sex. The men love buying cars from him too. When he confesses that "Personally, bro, I'm driving the new F-type and I love it," they often purchase the same model. Then as they drive off the lot they imagine being as young, vital and sexy as he is.

At fifty-three, with my hair thinning and my face drooping, I felt like an aging hound dog around Jake, and increasingly insecure about closing a deal.

A golfing friend of mine, Hal, at fifty-nine, recently had Botox shot into his forehead and reported feeling ten years younger. To me he looked a bit startled but clearly his mojo was on the rise. He said he was thinking about dermabrasion and hair plugs. I asked him what got him to take the plunge into face work. He said he wanted to get laid more. I said I was faithful to Ann but I wanted to sell more cars.

"Just as good a reason as any," he said, and gave me the name of his dermatologist.

In our twenty-odd years together, I had never kept a secret from Ann because there had never been a rea-son for one. But now, I knew what I wanted to do would upset my wife and possibly threaten our marriage. So I made an appointment for a consultation with Hal's dermatologist and told Ann I was getting my teeth cleaned.

Looking back I realize it was the beginning of our great divide. Sometimes it's another woman or another man and sometimes, it's lying about a cosmetic procedure. The thing that separates us from each other is not the particular details of betrayal but the concept of betrayal itself. Suddenly selling cars became more important to me then being honest with my wife. Vanity played a part, sure. I wanted to look younger and handsome again. Who wouldn't? And maybe avoiding death was running just beneath the surface of my mid-life choices.

Dr. Jhabvala said I had come just in time. We could laser my face, and inject collagen into my assorted wrinkles. "You will be very pleased, Mr. Matthews," he said and patted my shoulder like a cherished uncle.

"Will I sell more cars?" I half-joked.

"If that is what you want, it will be so," he smiled beautifully. He seemed more like a spiritual guide than a dermatologist.

Because my face could be red and swollen after the procedures, I told Ann I had to go to a three-day Jaguar conference in Las Vegas. When the nurse held up the mirror, I was shocked at how ghoulish I looked. Still, I went into work because I couldn't risk losing my job. With my low sales figures I was already on shaky ground. That week I sold no cars. Customers recoiled from me as if I had leprosy. Jake experienced the best week of his career. After work, I got take-out and holed up at a nearby Best Western drinking Bud and watching "Celebrity Apprentice."

When I returned home on day number four, Ann shouted, "What in the hell happened to you in Vegas? Did you get bitten by a tarantula or did you try to drink yourself to death?"

"I got sunburned is all, honey," I lied. "I fell asleep by the pool." She looked at me like I was insane. I vowed never to do another cosmetic procedure. It just wasn't worth the sneaking around.

Several months later, however, I ran into Hal at the hardware store. He'd had a complete facelift and looked fantastic. He said he was thrilled with the results. At fifty-nine, he was fucking like a twenty-year-old.

"How's the car business?" he asked.

I contacted his plastic surgeon, Dr. Pinch, and discussed an eyelift. A relatively minor surgery compared to a facelift, Dr. Pinch assured me, and far less expensive. "You're a perfect candidate," he declared, pointing out the excess puffs and folds of flesh above and below my eyes. "You'll heal in no time." He slapped my shoulder firmly, imprinting a guarantee of good results. I was nervous about the surgery, however minor, but even more nervous about what excuse to give Ann this time.

I came up with a visit to my sister Regina in Minnesota. "We haven't seen each other in five years and we're not getting any younger," I told Ann. She agreed it was a lovely thing for me to do. I felt guilty about lying but not guilty enough to tell the truth. Once again, I made reservations at our local Best Western.

According to Dr. Pinch, the procedure went splendidly. He was thrilled with himself. Still, I looked like a raccoon that had been in a fight with a black bear. In the recovery room, I asked the nurse how long it would take to heal. "Oh, the bruising should be gone in a few weeks," she answered. "Weeks? Dr. Pinch had made it sound like days," I said. "It varies, sweetie," she said cheerfully. "Be patient. You're going to look fabulous."

I couldn't hide from Ann for weeks, so I decided to go directly home and fess up. She might be pissed off at first but would get over it once the swelling went down and my car sales went up.

When I walked in the door, she screamed.

"Jesus Christ," she yelled. "What have you done to yourself now? Did you have a fucking facelift?"

"No, honey. Just an eyelift! I did it so I can sell more cars. I did it for us, love."

"I don't recognize you anymore!" she said. "We have totally different values." And she went into the bedroom and slammed the door. Hours later, she emerged to announce that she hadn't been happy for years and wanted a divorce.

My eyes healed and I looked better but not great. I was sad and nobody looks great when they're sad. I sold no more cars than I had before the surgery. I'd lost my wife and I was in danger of losing my job if I didn't start performing. What I needed was a radical change of attitude.

While playing golf with the newly invented Hal one Sunday, and discussing my protracted slump, he said, "Buddy, you should do the whole face. That will really get you where you want to go."

"You think so, huh?" I replied, and then without hesitation, I punched Hal squarely in his gorgeous $50,000 face.

The next day I sold three Jaguar XE convertibles.

Visiting Bobby

In this 1986 photograph, Bobby is thirty-six, wearing a tuxedo with a rainbow cummerbund, toasting with a glass of champagne as his lover of fifteen years, Russell, takes the winning shot. Bobby is at the top of his game, radiant, with an extravagant white smile, meticulously clipped black moustache, eyes flashing sapphire blue. Movie star handsome, with two years to live.

#

April 1, 1988. On the phone, Bobby's voice gallops, and in the background I can hear Bernstein's *Candide* blasting, which means he's feeling celebratory.

"Annie, I'm a new man. In the pink."

"All right, Bobby! Is it all those exotic animals you've been ingesting lately?"

"Absolutely. The squirrel's tail did the trick. Good as new." He's just on the other side of pneumocystis and a series of rashes and fevers the Chinese herbalist has been treating with pungent teas made from the entrails of snakes, turtles, lizards–who knows what–and needles three times a week. That plus the reishi mushrooms, silver probiotics, AZT and prayer–all attempts to kick HIV's ass.

"So, Gorgeous, let's make a date," I say. It's routine between us. His line is, "But what will your girlfriend say?" And I answer, "Honey, we just won't tell her."

"I have to come to Berkeley this week," he says. "I'm buying Paul the Claremont, so he won't have to stay with me."

"The Claremont what? The hotel?" I'm waiting for him to say "April Fools!" but he goes on in a serious tone.

"Yes! The hotel. It's in escrow. I got them to throw in the chef," he says. "I'll own most of Berkeley by Christmas."

Even though Paul, his younger brother, tells everyone not to support his fantasies because the doctor says it makes him crazier, I can't help but go along. It's a habit from the old days of our tongue-in-cheek bantering.

"How about the Greek Theater. Is that included?"

"Yes, that too, hon."

"Hey listen, I'm in SF tomorrow."

"Paul's here. Down from the mountain. He needed a change of scenery. Too much harmony. Come. We'll have a party."

The next day Paul delivers more of the doctor's advice. "We need to distract him like we would a child." He shrugs his shoulders, smiles with his lips held tight together. He resembles Bobby; you can tell they're brothers, especially around the eyes. "I've been chasing him all over the city. Last week he bought twenty refrigerators at Sears. I had to go in after him and cancel the order. It's like that twenty-four hours a day, one surprise after the other."

"You must be exhausted."

"I'm okay," he says, but looks haggard, a bit mad himself, bug-eyed, unshaven and pumped up with the extraordinary things being asked of him. "A couple of nights ago he was out at three in the morning, handing out hundred dollar bills to homeless people. He told them to clean up the city, then pissed in the street. Everything he used to do was funny. Now, nothing is." Paul leans on the table; his hands become a vise to hold up his head. He arrived two weeks ago after shutting down his construction business, and will stay indefinitely. His wife is at home with their two young children.

I rest my hand on his shoulder. "I'm here."

"I know," he says.

Bobby's condo overlooks the ocean near the Cliff House. The living room and kitchen are separated by a breakfast bar, creating an open entertainment space. Colorful rag rugs complement the bleached oak floors. Everything gay-tasteful and tidy. On the beveled glass coffee table is one of Bobby's flower arrangements of bright yellow tulips with blades of bear grass, travel books, stacks of photographs, a bowl of fruit, brownies, trail mix and loose change. It's sunny out, as it has been for weeks, with just enough wind to keep the skies a brilliant blue. The sliding glass door is open so you can hear the waves crashing, smell the salt air, catch the sweet perfume of freesias in full bloom in pots on the deck. No sign of illness, not a single bottle of pills. Bobby hides the AZT in the medicine cabinet. One day he showed me the bottle. "AZT. What do you think it stands for? A fraternity?"

Like myself, Bobby is a professional photographer. His walls are crowded with his personal favorite shots:

Harvey Milk in front of his camera store; Charles Pierce doing Bette Davis at the Plush Room; and a close-up of a marble, mausoleum-like toilet stall at I. Magnin's. Several portraits of friends, some gone, some still around.

Over the twenty years we've been friends, we've acted as each other's playmate as well as confidant, sharing our fantasies about unattainable bad boys and girls, or gushing the juicy details of a recent sexual escapade. More than once, we've dissolved into each other's arms over a trampled heart. Bobby always loved the baths, the drugs, the sex, reaching for the most bacchanal pleasure possible. Now those subjects are off limits and the ghostly romantic figures of his past have retreated to the dark shadows of wistful memory.

Bobby comes into the living room with a handful of photographs he lets fall like confetti onto the floor. His walk is slow, deliberate. In the month since I've last seen him, he's become a paler, thinner version of himself. Up close his skin is blotchy, his blue eyes ringed by shadow, but it's subtle decay, and if you didn't know, you might suspect he's just getting over the flu.

"I've started plans to renovate the windmills and resurrect the Sutro Baths. The workers will be here tomorrow."

"That's quite an undertaking, Mr. Slater." I smile.

"It's going to be fabulous." He smiles, heads for his study, then turns. "Don't worry, hon. I've hired the best. All women." Then he disappears down the hallway.

I get up from the couch and walk out onto the deck, take a few deep breaths of fresh air. It could be worse, I tell myself. I've seen much worse. Russell got mean, paranoid, after the retinopathy diagnosis. He started ordering everyone around, accusing them of stealing his money. Bobby is still so lovable and funny. What's the difference if his stories are make-believe? Isn't that a dying man's prerogative?

When I come back in, I sit on the floor, and look at photos Bobby's dumped there. There are several pictures taken in Provincetown the summer before Russell got sick. In one of them, Bobby and Russell are in skimpy swim trunks, standing near the breakwater at the tip of the Cape, waving at the camera. In another Bobby is pretending to pour his drink over Russell's head. They are gorgeous, muscular and tan, emanating the godlike youth and beauty every gay man envies.

Paul turns to me and lowers his voice, "It's bad, Annie, really bad. The doctors say there's nothing else they can do."

Bobby comes back in wearing a ski jacket and announces, "Come on, everyone. Let's go shopping."

In late May, Sarah, my girlfriend of eight years, and I take an early morning walk in Tilden Park. I'm restless, and can't even concentrate on the dazzling array of wildflowers, let alone Sarah's monologue about who-did-what-to-whom in her English department. When she notices that I'm distracted, she says: "Sweetie, maybe you should go see him today." So while Sarah grades essays, I make a gigantic pot of chicken soup and head for Bobby's oceanfront condo.

The elevator door slides open onto the fourth floor. Malcolm, Bobby's oldest friend from London, opens the door and kisses my cheek. His presence is further evidence that Bobby is very ill.

"Hi, Annie. Come in. He's expecting you, love."

"Chicken soup," I say, handing the pot to Malcolm.

"It's hard to believe," he whispers. "Last summer he ran me ragged." Malcolm looks rugged and healthy, as do most of Bobby's friends and ex-lovers. Until they don't.

In the living room, Bobby is sitting up on the couch, dressed in one of his designer cashmere sweaters, eating a bagel. He's bone thin, and the wisps of hair on his head fly out like ethereal conduits.

"Welcome to Robert Slater's Rehabilitation Center." He waves me in. "Have a bagel, kid."

"You're looking dapper today, like a talk show host." I kiss the top of his head, then sit beside him on the couch.

"Are you my first guest?" he asks.

"No interviews until I've eaten something." Reaching for a bagel, I notice Paul sitting quietly on the love seat facing us, folding laundry, and Malcolm in a wicker chair near the outside deck, mending a pair of Bobby's pants.

Picking up the Princess phone, Bobby dials a couple of digits. "Send over fifty Oriental lamps," he says. "Yes, today. I've got a client waiting here. Make that before lunch." He winks and hangs up, breathing heavily. Paul had disconnected this phone the night before, but Bobby doesn't seem to have noticed. He just keeps dialing, ordering things, and hanging up. He lifts the receiver again, stares at it, and places it back on the cradle. "I'm leaving for China in the morning. On a shoot for National Geographic. Want to come along Annie? Everything's paid for."

I look for Paul. He's putting towels away in the linen closet. "Sure, Bobby. Share the credits?"

"Deal," he says, shaking my hand. "You drive a hard bargain." Coughing a few times, he excuses himself to the bathroom.

"Yesterday he was in a tropical mood." Malcolm looks up from his sewing and smiles. "He phoned Sloat Gardens and ordered every palm tree they had, then he rang up the Galleria to buy twenty rattan couches for the condos he's buying all of us. So we can have our own little commune." Malcolm winks. Then he tears up and his face flushes red.

Bobby limps back into the living room. He drops a camera and a flashlight onto the coffee table and lets out a sigh. "I've got to get over there tonight and check the lighting," he says to Malcolm, who nods, as if to say, consider it done.

"Don't worry," Bobby says to me, "I'm buying you a condo, too. TV, microwave, Jacuzzi, the works. It's all taken care of. But, you have to bring your own bed."

"My own bed?"

"Yes, love," he says, squinting, then loses his balance and falls back onto the couch. "And linens," he whispers, losing his breath.

Paul touches Bobby's hand. "How about some tea, Bobby? Everyone?" He disappears into the kitchen.

Lying on the couch, Bobby holds a finger out in front of him, studying a broken nail from every angle, as though his life depends on it.

At home that night, I sit at the piano and look at his photograph of a year before, then imagine him as he is now with all the minute changes in between that alter a physical body irrevocably. I go back and forth between then and now dozens of times until I fall asleep sitting up, and Sarah wakes me to get me into bed.

Two weeks later, I get a call from Paul. "Would you mind coming over, Annie? Bobby's been crying all morning. He's taking it pretty hard about Malcolm leaving."

When I arrive at the condo, Paul is slumped on the couch staring at Gorbachev on the cover of Time. Bobby's in grey and white striped pajamas, trying to set the table. He's moved his latest flower arrangement of white roses from the coffee table to one of the dining room chairs. The condo feels lonely, empty without Malcolm. I wish more people were around to tell stories and jokes. Social banter temporarily camouflages grief.

"You're just in time," Bobby says. He seems confused about where utensils belong, but perseveres. "It's so hard to get good help these days. I had to fire Malcolm this morning. He kept dropping things."

"Oh. Malcolm's gone back to London?"

"No. No. He'll be here for dinner. Set a place for him."

I smile and touch his cheek. I'm very close to him now and can see tiny crumbs of food caught in the stubble of his beard.

His mouth opens, twitches with the possibility of humor, but it's as if words get lost down a black hole in his throat. Unsteady on his feet, he hands me placemats and linen napkins. A fork dangles from his fingers for several seconds before it falls to the floor. He looks down at it. I kneel and pick it up.

"Found it," I say, stupidly, trying to maintain a sense of play.

"We're having twelve for lunch. David Bowie is coming, so let's make it pretty, hon. We don't want to disappoint Malcolm."

"Can we fit twelve at this table, Bobby?"

"I've had fifty people at this table," he says. "Anyway, the others can eat on the floor. Come see my latest remodeling project." With shaky fingers, he clutches my hand and leads me into the living room. He's been tearing out the wall nearest the deck with a croquet mallet. "Opening up space," he says. I stare at the guts of the wall, exposed wires, insulation, and a deep hollowness that is the belly beneath the hammered sheet rock.

"Interesting," I say.

"I'm going to knock out the bedroom wall, too," he tells me, confidentially. He seems pleased with my attentiveness. "The view will be better. I don't think Paul likes the idea. He keeps putting things back the way they were. But what does he know?" He leans on me, a substitute for a hug. "To tell you the truth," he continues with a finger to his lips, "Paul's been acting pretty crazy lately. Living up on that mountain, all that air, and so many trees you can't see the road. He doesn't know what's going on in the City. I'm a little worried about him. I'm sending him home with my stress-reduction books. And you!" He pats my hand. "You can read them here." He laughs, then picks up a camera and scans the horizon, clicks a few times, first in the direction of the ocean, then at a lamp, and finally snaps one of his own photographs.

In late July, when I peek into his study, he's in a black velour bathrobe, bent over his desk, staring at a single framed photograph. It's an idyllic pastoral scene of sheep traveling over rolling green hills toward the ocean at sunset, white puffs of clouds suspended above a winding path down to the blue sea. Bobby took this photo some years ago when he and Russell were hiking in Scotland, sending their friends bragging postcards about their treacherous ten- to twelve-mile hikes. On the floor around Bobby are piles of papers, books, photos, an Avedon-framed print of Nureyev in flight, sweaters and catalogues, some with pages torn out and scattered on the rug, all mingling with dirty underwear, crumpled dollar bills, coins, and a half eaten bowl of oatmeal with bananas and raisins.

"How you doing, kiddo?" I say.

"Excellent," he answers, but doesn't look up. His attention has shifted to Nureyev. It's as if he doesn't have neck muscles to lift his head. Paul comes in to check on him to make sure he hasn't fallen. He acknowledges my presence with a warm smile and nod, then exits. I watch the clock, waiting for Bobby to speak. But he stares at Nureyev until he folds up on the carpet and goes to sleep.

On the way to my car, I realize I've forgotten my jacket. When I go back upstairs, the door is open and I walk in. Paul is sitting alone on the deck, looking out to sea. As I get closer I hear him sobbing. I grab my jacket, back up quietly, wait a minute, then tiptoe out. We have gone beyond the place where we can comfort each other, imprisoned as we are within the walls of our own fear.

Two friends from New York dropped by for a few hours earlier today and another guy I've never met from L.A. is expected tomorrow. It's a bright August afternoon and we've got the sliding glass door wide open to capture the warm, summer air before the fog rolls in. Right now in the living room it's just Bobby, Paul, and me. Paul has been darting in and out all afternoon –mails a letter, comes back with Ajax and sponges, goes jogging, hauls in bags of groceries and tools to fix this or that. Currently he's sitting apart from us at the bar, doing a crossword puzzle, taking a timeout. Mostly Bobby sleeps or mumbles strange combinations of words. Still, in the silences, I can't help but listen for a witty remark, a comeback.

After a long, fidgety silence, Paul snaps his fingers. "Cicada. That's it. A six-letter word for singing insect."

"Ah, cicadas." Bobby opens his eyes. "Remember the old days in Chicago, Pauly?"

"Yeah. Those cicadas sure make a racket in the summertime."

"Yes, they do," Bobby smiles and pulls a blanket up to his chin.

"Are you warm enough, pal?" Paul says. Bobby nods his head up and down slowly. "I can get you another blanket."

"No. Thank you, hon." Bobby smiles at his brother. "You get some rest. You've been working too hard." Then his eyes close.

Paul looks at me. "Cicadas are amazing, all right. They lay their eggs, then the larva burrows four to five feet underground and seventeen years later, the adults come out, mate, lay their eggs and die."

"I haven't been in the mood lately," Bobby rolls his eyes, "but I might be in seventeen years." We all laugh. Then Paul goes back to his puzzle. Bobby seems to be dozing, then suddenly sits up, wide-eyed passionate. "I dipped the shells of two cicadas in gold to make you that gilded necklace. I sent it in the Chinese box, remember?" he says to Paul. Paul looks up.

"No, I don't remember, Bobby."

"Well you better find it. It's very valuable."

Paul rubs his hands through his hair, sighs, then gets up and goes into the kitchen.

"I remember," I lie.

"Extremely delicate work. It won a prize, you know."

"I'm not surprised." Bobby blows me a kiss.

"The necklace is in the trunk of your car," Bobby shouts to Paul, which comes out as a loud whisper. "Go get it."

"There's no necklace in my car, Bobby," Paul yells back. "There's no necklace."

"What do you know? You don't know anything about me. You haven't seen me in years."

Paul flinches. "I've been here for weeks, Bobby. I see you all the time."

"No," Bobby insists, his eyes teary. He raises his voice and veins stand out on his pale forehead. "No. No. No. It's been seventeen years," and he turns his head away. Paul slams drawers, bangs cabinets, opens the refrigerator.

"You know, Annie," Bobby whispers secretly to me, as if I'm the only one left who understands him. "Russell's coming tonight. He called and said, `This is Russell.' `Russell who?' I said just to make sure, you know. 'I'm coming over tonight,' he said. 'Should I bring something?' I told him just bring yourself. That's more than enough."

"Absolutely," I say, listening carefully, but also watching Paul in the kitchen leaning over the sink, washing lettuce. The loud running water creates a curtain between us.

"Boy, when he walked in, well, it was really something. He's been dead for so long, it was very emotional for me to see him alive again." His voice cracks and falters.

"I bet it was. I know how much you loved Russell."

Bobby lifts his bony hand in the air, and I watch it, graceful as a bird in flight, travel slowly toward me. He takes my hand and squeezes hard, harder than I imagined he could.

"I'll be right back," he says. He lifts himself by gripping the arm of the couch, then hobbles, leaning on pieces of furniture to get where's he's going. His arms and legs are sticks. I watch Paul wince as he follows Bobby's trek with his eyes. When Paul returns to the living room, his face is drained of anger; he simply looks sad when he says, "Guess that's it. Probably gone to bed."

"He said he'd be right back." Suddenly I'm panicked at the thought of him not returning.

We sit in silence, waiting. I pick up the latest Photography and flip through the dramatic images while Paul stares into space.

A few minutes later, Bobby limps back into the room, using the cane Paul got him weeks ago, which he's refused to use until tonight. Over his free arm is draped a white silk kimono. He smiles and hands it to me.

"Exquisite, Bobby. Where'd you get it?" I run my hands along the slippery, silk texture.

"Try it on, hon," he says. "It's you." He leans on the arm of the couch, one hip cocked, an eyebrow raised.

"Really?"

"Come on. Come on. Put it on." Paul, looking exhausted, walks into the bedroom and shuts the door. I look up at Bobby. The robe he's worn all week has soup stains down the front. Beneath the black velour, his spindly legs are stark white, hard like ivory, not flesh. I hesitate. "Put it on," he coaxes. "Look who's here! Show Russell what it looks like on a real girl." Then he collapses on the couch beside me. He looks adoringly at the empty place beside him on the couch where Russell's ghost is waiting for the show.

I rise. I put on the kimono. Bobby waves his finger in a small, slow circle, so I turn around and around, ham it up like a fashion model, even bow a couple of times. I give him my best performance.

"Enough." he says, using his hands some more, something like a conductor marking time. "Time to sit down now."

I sit, resting my empty hands on the folds of silk in my lap. The kimono, the shell that once held Bobby, smooth and cool on my shoulders, flowing down around my wrists and ankles. I stroke it for comfort. I keep my head down. Too heavy to lift. The fog is in and the night air begins to chill my bones as I watch the whiteness of the gown become snow, then an icy, blinding light. I am frozen, almost serene in the complete stillness. If I don't move, I won't feel him leaving.

About the Author

Susan's work has appeared in *Amelia, Ascent, Christopher Street, the Feminist Art Journal, Narrative Magazine, the Patterson Literary Review, Paris Transcontinental, Yellow Silk* and *in Juked.* She is a frequent contributor to the *San Francisco Chronicle* and the *Funny Times.* She is the author of *Walking Vanilla,* a novel, and the editor of *This Is Women's Work,* an anthology. Susan was awarded a Marin Arts Council Individual Writers Grant in 2003 for her short fiction, "The Ozzie and Harriet Factor."

Susan Isa Efros lives in Marin County with Jerilyn Gilbert, her partner of 30 years. Contact her at susanefros.com

Made in the USA
Columbia, SC
27 September 2020

21571776R00137